BLINDSIDE

ALSO BY JIM R. LANE

DUTY

BLINDSIDE

A NOVEL

Jim R. Lane

BRIDGE WORKS PUBLISHING COMPANY

Bridgehampton, New York

Published by Bridge Works Publishing Company, Bridgehampton, New York, a member of the Rowman & Littlefield Publishing Group.

Distributed in the United States by National Book Network, Lanham, Maryland. For descriptions of this and other Bridge Works books, visit the National Book Network website at www.nbnbooks.com.

FIRST EDITION

The characters and events in this book are fictitious. Any similarity to actual persons, living or dead, is coincidental and not intended by the author.

Library of Congress Cataloging-in-Publication Data

Lane, Jim R.
    Blindside : a novel / Jim R. Lane.—1st ed.
        p. cm.
    ISBN 1-882593-59-6 (hardcover : alk. paper)
    1. United States. Navy—Fiction.   2. Courts-martial and courts of inquiry—Fiction.   3. Trials (Adultery)—Fiction.   I. Title.
    PS3562.A484415 B57   2002
    813'.54—dc21   2002003370

                    10 9 8 7 6 5 4 3 2 1

For Wendolina, who got me into this.

This is his first punishment, that by the verdict of his own heart, no guilty man is acquitted.
—Juvenal

My deep appreciation to those who never failed to show their enthusiam for this book. To my agent and friend Wendy Dager; to literary consultant and confidant Jacquelyn Powers; and to Alexandra Shelley, whose hard-nosed edits improved the story immeasurably. And love and thanks to my Pam, the best wife a writer could have.

BLINDSIDE

CHAPTER ONE

Neal Olen felt damn stupid standing in line. His hand was perspiring, dampening the slick blue and pink dust jacket on *Navy Wench*. It was not the sort of novel he'd normally buy, but this was the only way he could get close enough to her now. Two armed guards who wore the tough-ass demeanor of off-duty city police, rather than civilian rent-a-cops, had stepped in his way when he tried to approach the table where Angela Vance sat signing her novel. So he muttered a confused apology, paid for the damned thing, and got in the sluggish line. He'd had enough of lines in the navy. Even as an officer he hadn't been able to escape the perennial lines for mail, meals and medicine. He opened the book in his hand, thumbing pages randomly, stopping at the occasional paragraph that caught his eye.

The guards spoke quietly with each other, standing with thumbs hooked over belts, keeping a not-too-subtle eye on him. Neal lowered the novel and gazed idly away, trying to avoid looking furtive. He noted the warm fragrance the in-house coffee bar added to the cavernous Thousand Oaks bookstore. Neal glanced back at the cops, exhaling his

1

frustration. They probably had him pegged for a celebrity stalker. He wondered if he fit some police profile: 5' 10", 160 pounds, hair: brown, eyes: brown, quiet, nervous—maybe what the cops call *shifty*. His hand rose involuntarily, fingers lightly touching the inch-long scar above his left eyebrow. The wound, received in childhood from his older brother and inexpertly sutured at the county hospital, was one of the identifying marks listed in his military service record. The scar, along with the angular line of his jaw, made him ruggedly handsome in his wife's generous assessment. He never thought about his facial topography except when she happened to bring it up or at times like these, when such physical imperfections made him easily identifiable to the police.

Neal had heard about the book and Angela Vance, but he had not even imagined he might have some part in it until he'd caught her public television interview on *Story Line* last Thursday night. She was promoting her book and mentioned an unnamed "navy hero" who had been valuable in her research. Now, five weeks after its release, *Navy Wench* was already a best-seller and had been featured in *Newsweek* alongside an article about military readiness in the new millennium. Buzz about the novel had shown up in other places as well: newspaper book reviews, magazines, online booksellers. The book had even been optioned for a movie. Angela Vance had been pegged by *People* magazine as someone to watch in the year 2000 and beyond. Now Angela had received her twenty minutes in front of *Story Line*'s national audience, answering even the most inane questions with a dazzling smile and another mention of the book title.

Neal had been startled when *Story Line*'s host, Gene Klassen, wearing his most serious face, had asked about apparently classified information contained in *Navy Wench*. "I've got my sources," she answered coyly. Angela Vance had clearly enchanted Klassen, a normally hard-nosed interviewer, just as she had mesmerized Neal back in Coronado at the Old Tijuana Restaurant bar.

Neal had to learn details of what in hell she had written and, more importantly, had to remember what he might have said to her, even accidentally, that could land him in federal prison. For a navy intelligence officer, nighttime intimacies could inspire the male need to show off by spilling secrets.

Neal was once again thinking defensively, analytically, winnowing every detail from available data, a habit left over from twenty years as a navy intelligence officer with assignments at U.S. embassies, aboard ships and ashore with navy and NATO commands. Then, he had concentrated on developing threat assessments and briefing admirals and ambassadors. Neal had been thoroughly happy in his role as an office spook, a paperwork spy.

He never could have conceived that the sleazy tell-all novel he held in his hand would interest him, let alone affect him personally. Now, as Neal stood in line, he imagined that people were stealing glances at him, could actually see him naked four years earlier in the old hotel in the Laguna Mountains with Angela's lip prints all over him. He flashed on the several lines he'd seen quoted in a review of *Navy Wench* and its *fictional* characters.

Allen Neil lay back, spent, as Gillian Lorenz nuzzled close, taking little nips at his ear, her hand languidly cupping his penis, clearly not finished with him. Now he had a lucid moment, time to think, to consider whether he should have bragged to her about the KH-11 reconnaissance satellites. Damn! No question about it—he had fucked up royally.

A queasy feeling had come over him again, just as when he'd seen her interviewed on television. Angela Vance, vamping for the camera, hinting at Neal's hidden shame, the "intimate wink" that characterized her book promotion. She'd revealed a version of her own life and the lives of those whom she somehow found amusing and useful to her story and, now, useful to its sales.

Since the book had hit the stores little more than a month ago, some of the women at the office had been acting strangely, whispering and giggling whenever he came near, like children with a secret. They had obviously put some clues together. The female attention would have been a kick any other time—like the day Sheila, the office tart, had patted his ass at the Xerox machine. But now he hoped fervently that none of them would see him here. That would clinch it for them, make his connection to Angela Vance undeniable. Forget the logic that if there had been any permanent intimacy going on between them, she would not have embarrassed him by making him wait in the autograph line.

Neal had resisted his initial impulse to buy a copy of *Navy Wench*. But then he had seen the ad for Angela Vance's promotional book signing in the *Los Angeles Times*. Just a fifteen-minute drive up the Ventura Freeway to Thousand Oaks from his house in Camarillo. He had imagined the book-signing scene differently, without the reverent herd of mostly women autograph seekers in a line snaking through the bookstore. He wondered if Angela Vance would recognize his face now that she had attained enough fame to warrant a pair of guards. She'd remembered other things about him—that was for damned sure—if the Allen Neil character was supposed to be based on him.

He could hear her laugh from his position back in the line. He recognized that brash, ready, too-loud laugh that would not normally have attracted him. It was unashamed, nearly a shriek, the kind that rose above the noise in a busy restaurant. He had heard her laugh the first time in Coronado, when he'd already had a couple of drinks and was feeling lonely, guilty and also furious that his wife, Yvonne, had asked him to move out.

Neal stepped to the side and peered down the line of twenty Angela Vance fans in front of him. Her legs, crossed at the knee, were visible under the table—one high heel planted in the carpet, the other moving slightly up and down, maintaining some inner rhythm as she autographed each book. A green silk blouse sleeve and that red hair were all he could see of her above the table as she bent forward to scratch her name and some phony personal message to anyone who had the $29.95 for her book. She looked up after each autograph, smiling, revealing her carefully made-up face, giving full value to the book buyer's brush with her radiance.

AT THE TIME OF HIS separation from his wife, Neal had only a little over three years to retirement. Despite Yvonne's impatience for him to retire, how could he throw away the sixteen years he—they—had already invested? Besides, he had one of the navy's best jobs as an intelligence officer and had just been promoted to O-5—commander. Not that Neal would ever admit out loud that it mattered, but replacing his plain-billed lieutenant commander cap with one that carried embroidered gold oak leaves, "scrambled eggs," on the visor had made him stand a bit taller and sneak an occasional look in the mirror, like a Little Leaguer on uniform day.

Two weeks after Yvonne had asked him to move out of their San Diego home, he had rented an apartment over a garage in Coronado, chauffeur's quarters built in the '20s. It was quiet, furnished, lonely. He could have lived aboard the USS *Constellation*, moored at North Island's carrier pier, but booze was not allowed aboard, and he'd been using more of it these days. He needed a space of his own other than the small stateroom on the ship's O-3 level, just beneath the flight deck. Neal had already spent plenty of time in that windowless steel box during cruises.

So Neal celebrated his promotion alone, sitting in the Old Tijuana, contemplating the chunks of salt sliding down his margarita glass, when this dish in a gauzy skirt perched herself just one stool away. What now? Buy her a drink? Strike up a conversation? Pretend like she isn't there, he decided. He glanced down, catching sight of her knee and a generous wedge of thigh pointing his way as she turned on the stool to wave at someone across the room. Neal looked up and directly into her face. She looked back, staring a moment before breaking a smile, showing her teeth. Good teeth, television teeth, like in a toothpaste ad. They were the kind of teeth that made you think of your own and keep your mouth shut.

"It's OK—you can talk," she said, leaning close, eyes wide as her smile.

"Must be out of practice," was all he could think to say. *Dumb.*

"That can only mean that you're married."

"Separated," he said too quickly. "I mean—"

"Separated is OK," she said, reaching across the empty stool between them, giving his knee a quick pat. "Lots of sailors are, honey." She gazed at him, appraising, then extended her hand to shake. "Angela," she said.

Fast mover, he thought, encouraged but wary. It was the way foreign agents sometimes approached military people, and it set off an alarm in the back of his mind. And as an intelligence officer he'd be a prime target with his high-level clearances and broad knowledge of up-to-date classified information. It could make a guy paranoid.

"I'm Neal." He knew better than to ask how she knew he was navy. Add it up: right age, dorky haircut, navy town. At least he wasn't wearing shiny black shoes and khaki pants.

"Care for a drink?" he said, as she slid onto the stool next to him.

NEAL TOOK A BLANK slip of paper from a table near where Angela sat signing. He'd seen some of the others in line use the slip to write out their names for Angela. Neal wrote: "I have to see you when you're done here. Black Angus bar next door." He slipped the paper inside the dust jacket, sticking out. He turned the book over and read the blurbs. *The navy under covers. What really happens when sailors leave home . . . . Not since the Tailhook scandal. . . .*

Tailhook. The chance that Angela Vance's seamy revelations would be ignored, just forgotten, seemed less and less likely with the prevailing attitude that had engulfed any civilian discussion of the navy. The Tailhook scandal had moved the military and its archaic attitudes about women and sex front and center before the public. And the clank of brass had been deafening as senior officers dived for cover at the merest suggestion of sexual impropriety.

Neal's turn came. Angela looked up with the same dazzling smile and moist brown eyes he remembered from the first night he'd seen her in the Old Tijuana. No hint of surprise. "Nice to see you again, Neal," she said without hesitation. "How's my hero?"

"Congratulations. I hear the book's doing well." Neal faked a cheery demeanor, mindful of the cops now standing close, eyes locked on him.

"Twenty-two on the *Times* best-seller list," she said, with that prominent laugh coloring her words. She withdrew the slip, glanced at it, then bent over Neal's copy of *Navy Wench* and wrote, "To Neal Olen, more love and kisses from a hero worshipper."

Closing the cover on his note, she slid the book across the table toward him. He searched her eyes for an answer, but they had suddenly lost luster and expression, had gone private. He'd just have to wait at the bar. It would give him time to start reading the book in earnest, to assess the damage she had done him. The signing would end at 4 P.M.

The Black Angus was nearly deserted on this Saturday afternoon. Heavy metal music pounded through the speakers. The hostess, noting the book in his hand, led him to a table that had light from a window. "Good book," she said, nodding as Neal slipped into one of the four captain's chairs. "Been next door, huh? She still there?"

"Yeah," Neal answered and ordered a gin and tonic.

"You gonna read, I'll turn down the music," she said. He flashed her a smile of appreciation. "I was married to a sailor once. . . ." The hostess gave him a knowing nod, looking for a response, and, receiving none, turned away.

Neal opened *Navy Wench*, took a sip of his gin and tonic, and began reading, quickly realizing that the book's slant was anything but friendly to the sea service. Angela Vance's novel was very clearly written from an angry woman's point of view, told through the protagonist, Gillian Lorenz, an abused and promiscuous navy wife. Gillian's philandering enlisted husband was abetted in his whore-mongering by cruises aboard his ship to the western Pacific where he "dipped his wick in every hooker from Olongapo City to Pattaya Beach to Mombassa."

He closed the book and his eyes. It was only sex, he kept telling himself. But Neal Olen knew that what would be considered an indiscretion anywhere else had the potential in the navy to ruin him. His only hope was that now that he had been retired from the navy for nearly a year, the furor might bypass him.

CHAPTER TWO

"Eighty-five," Angela Vance said, startling Neal. She stood across his table, close enough for him to catch her scent. She wore one of those perfumes that sounded like it might burn your skin to put it on, something like Opium or Poison. "You'll find what you're looking for starting on page eighty-five," she repeated when he didn't respond. Angela slipped into the chair opposite. "That *is* what you're here about, isn't it." Not a question.

"Care to tell me why?" His voice was carefully metered, without expression.

That laugh again from perfectly painted lips. "Sales, Neal, why else? Sales, money, fame. A house on Glorietta Bay. Something wrong with that?"

"But why make it so obvious—why stick it to me in a television interview? Why make those references to a real 'navy hero' who inspired one of your characters?"

"I'm stuck at twenty-two on the best-sellers, Neal, and I need to jog it loose. Besides, what's the difference, even if you're recognized? I can think of thousands of men who'd love to be linked to me." She touched her hair in a mocking, beauty-queen gesture. "You've won the stud-of-the-week sweepstakes. You got into Angela Vance's skivvies. Don't mention to anyone it was before my skivvies got famous."

"You're willing to drop a bomb on my life to move your book?" He felt his neck prickling.

"Neal, darling, it's my livelihood."

He said nothing. What could he say to her that would make any difference?

"According to my publisher I shouldn't expect *Wench* to go much further. It's already past the initial excitement phase." Now a businesswoman was speaking. "I may not get a bump this time from the hero thing, but it'll definitely do wonders for my next book. Builds my credibility. I could use a drink." She crossed her legs, making it clear she expected someone else to fetch it. Neal didn't move. "These signings wear me out. All that grinning and graciousness. Every one of those women in line just has to tell me their own story. Let 'em write their own book."

"Cuba Libre," Angela said when the cocktail waitress approached.

"Look, it's nothing personal, Neal. I write what I know, or what I can find out. I know about getting screwed by the navy—and others. The hero thing was just my good luck. It isn't in the book, if that's what you're worried about—the manuscript was in galleys by the time you became famous. It was too late to change the page proofs without costing the publisher extra money. Besides, it didn't really matter. It didn't have to be in the book for me to mention it on talk shows." Her expression asked for his understanding of the difficulties she faced. "I didn't even know about it until I saw them showing you off in Washington. You looked darling all dressed up in your uniform."

"It's been four years since we met in Coronado," Neal said. "I was separated, but now I'm back together with my wife and things are working out. I don't need this shit from you."

"You're making too much of it, Neal. What's a little nooky on the side when you got no home to go to? I seem to recall you living in a garage at the time, like some kind of crazy uncle. I thought you were cute but tight-assed—both definitions." She leaned to one side to make her inspection. "Your hair's better now, but you really should see a stylist. Besides, how do you know your wife wasn't doing the dirty with the fleet while you were doing me?"

Neal felt his anger rise another notch, instantly deciding the time had come to leave, before he said or did something else he'd regret even more. He stood and became aware of the blue uniforms stirring in response three tables away. He hadn't seen the guards from the bookstore come in. He stared at them pointedly and then turned to Angela, fixing her image in his memory. She looked back, smiling, giving a momentary shrug, raising her Cuba Libre in a silent toast. "You don't know, Neal, do you? What do you think happens when you go to sea?"

Neal clamped his lips, turned and walked stiff-legged past the guards and into the southern California sunshine.

NEAL DROVE AUTOMATICALLY down Highway 101 toward Camarillo and home, paying cursory attention to traffic thickened with early Christmas shoppers. His mind wrestled with the past and his reluctance to embrace the events in Hawaii that had changed so much. The *hero thing* Angela had called it, making it sound like a movie special effect. He'd do it again if faced with the same situation, though Angela's knowledge of that one act was now the catalyst for his ruin. And no one was going to dive in to save him. Everything about his own instant celebrityhood had been too fast, too uncontrollable.

NEAL WOULD HAVE BEEN happy flying over to Maui from Honolulu and renting a car, but Yvonne had grown attached to their old blue Miata and had worked the car ferry between Oahu and Maui into their vacation plan. The slow ride on the old ship would be romantic, she had said, like it would be driving the roadster with the top down around Maui.

Diesel exhaust from the ferry's engines gave the sea air pungency. The cars in the group waiting to board were waved down the pier, across the ramp, and onto the ferry by a deckhand. They staggered the vehicles along both sides the length of the open tunnel-like cargo area, leaving space down the middle. Neal and Yvonne left the Miata for the observation deck above, climbing a narrow stairway. They bought iced tea from the snack bar and settled into a pair of deck chairs for the half-day cruise to the southeastern island.

Neal took Yvonne's hand and gave the fingers a kiss. She smiled at the gesture and held up her other hand to his face. He grinned and gave that one a kiss too.

Things had gotten measurably better between them. The two-year rebuilding effort since Neal's transfer to Hawaii, when they had agreed to try patching up their marriage, had shown results. Neal felt more relaxed, laughing more, taking life as it came. This vacation was proof. Their marriage seemed to have survived his career, and in a few months that pressure would be off as he completed this tour and transferred to the fleet reserve, in effect retiring.

Neal leaned back in the deck chair and closed his eyes against the sun as the ferry lurched away from the pier. Yvonne had been pushing Neal to leave the navy almost from the day they had married, when he had been a lieutenant junior grade. That was twenty years ago. As a child and the daughter of an air force master sergeant, Yvonne had hated the family's moves. Yet, though tears filling her blue eyes was her first response to every new set of transfer orders, the willowy blond child had the emotional capacity to quickly dispose of her anguish, surrendering fatalistically, withdrawing from school and the other children. She found solace in ballet training. It had become the single constant in her life. Yvonne had been sixteen, and a graceful five-foot-seven, when, landing from a *grande jeté*, she had twisted her right foot, rolling it painfully on its outside edge. Complications in healing left Yvonne with a lifelong limp.

With Neal, she liked the exotic assignments ashore—Italy and the Bahamas. The exciting locales made living with their childless marriage tolerable, if still imperfect. A failed pregnancy and subsequent surgery had left her infertile. With his final sea-duty assignment on the USS *Constellation*, their partnership had shown signs of weakening further under the strain of his being away months on end. The Hawaii assignment had changed that.

Neal opened his eyes and looked at his wife as she read a Maui travel brochure. Love and contentment dominated his thoughts as he dozed off.

"KIMO!" A WOMAN'S SCREAM topped the ship's engine noise as the ferry climbed a deep, swelling roller head-on. They were about an hour out of Honolulu. Neal instantly stood, alert—as he would be to general quarters sounding on a warship. The woman's scream had come from below. A wheelchair containing a child, strapped in, careened between the cars down the tilted deck toward the stern ramp. The chair struck the restraining chain across the opening at its lowest point, catching the footrests, driving the chair forward in its momentum. The wheelchair hesitated, hanging inverted with its occupant for a moment, then as the ship pitched forward on the backside of the swell, it dropped off the ramp, disappearing into the sea below the stern.

"Tell the captain!" Neal yelled to Yvonne. Grabbing a life ring from the bulkhead, he dashed aft. He leaped the wooden cap rail, falling thirty feet into the churning wake below, thrusting the life ring to arm's length a moment before his feet touched ocean.

He came quickly to the surface, swimming down the ship's wake at the best speed he could muster. The hull's passing left a bubble trail and temporarily flat water, but the ocean would soon erase the white wake, returning the surface chop that would camouflage anyone in the water. Neal swam a lifesaving crawl, keeping his head above water so he could keep his eye on the wheelchair, which was barely floating, sustained by air trapped in the seat and back cushions and in the vinyl gym bag tied between the handles. The boy's small head, black hair floating on the sea, lolled back. He made an uncoordinated effort to swim, hands slapping the water without force or direction—a rag doll's effort.

Neal felt the burn of brine in his throat. As he swam in the four-foot chop, he lost sight of the boy momentarily. The chair was sinking, cushions and gym bag rapidly losing air. He held the life ring lanyard, letting the red and white circular float trail behind where it would not hamper the power of his arm strokes and kicks. Neal reached the chairbound boy a moment after he slipped beneath the surface. Neal dove under, grasping the gym bag—the closest object—hauling it and the occupied wheelchair upward with effort. He broke the surface and caught his first blurred look at a crying, sputtering face in the water beside him. The boy gasped and went under, the weight of the wheelchair dragging him down once more.

Neal dove with him and clawed for the buckle of the strap that held the boy in the seat. Finding the clasp beneath the boy's billowing shirt, he yanked the buckle release and the wheelchair fell away, headed rapidly for the sea floor of the Kaiwi Channel.

At the ocean surface Neal hauled in the life ring and pulled it over the boy's head and arms, supporting the limp, painfully thin body. The nut-brown face contorted in fear and confusion. The child made low wailing sounds, flopping his arms uselessly. *That's good*, Neal thought. *He's alive and hasn't swallowed too much water*. Neal had qualified in artificial respiration and CPR, but that had been on dry land—pretty much useless in the water where he could find nothing solid to brace against. He kept a hand on the life ring and a grip on the boy's shirt while ripping his own shirt off with the other. Neal could swing his white shirt as a signal for lookouts on the ferry, sure to be searching for them in the growing seas.

Hawaiian water was warm even where the open ocean swept between the islands. Hypothermia wouldn't be a problem yet. They could last out here for several hours, but Neal deeply believed, had to believe, that it would be no more than minutes. The life ring was not meant for two, in either its flotation capacity or its configuration. It would take some effort, some swimming, to keep it stable, and he would have to swim for them both.

There had been plenty of witnesses on board the ferry—not like being lost in a plane crash in a lonely ocean with no help nearby. Yvonne would make sure the ship turned, he told himself—or scratch out the captain's eyes and do it herself. *Meanwhile*, he thought, *I've got to calm the boy and try not to imagine sharks below. Big surf and sharks—what the Kaiwi Channel is known for.*

"Is your name Kimo?" he asked. The child stopped moaning, recognition coming into his eyes. He coughed, bringing up seawater, eyes tearing. Neal put a hand on Kimo's head, smoothing the black hair, smiling. "Don't worry, Kimo. Won't be long now. They're coming for us." Neal gasped, heart pounding with the effort of his swim and the proximity of death.

"Kimo, ever hear the song about Barnacle Bill the Sailor?"

The child's eyes widened though he said nothing. "Who's that knocking at my door—" Neal began in a tuneless voice. His reward was a mouthful of saltwater and a grin on Kimo's lips.

NEAL TRIED TO MAINTAIN a normal demeanor once home from his trip to the Thousand Oaks bookstore. Yet he couldn't manage to make small talk over dinner with Yvonne. Asked, he blamed his quiet on thinking about work, then retreated to the den for the evening to consider what the fallout from *Navy Wench* might be. Yvonne watched a PBS nature show in the living room.

Later, she leaned against the den doorframe. "Coming to bed?" Yvonne Olen had already changed into a T-shirt that revealed the lower curve of her bare buttocks when she moved. At forty-two, she still stayed in shape, though it took greater effort than before and she tended to favor the foot she had injured as a girl. Standing five-seven and weighing one-twenty-five, she cut a trim figure.

He had first seen the twenty-one-year-old Yvonne across the white marble counter of her teller position. The bank job had supported her during her final year at San Diego State. It had first been no more than friendly banter while she processed his deposit. He watched, fascinated, as her slender fingers caressed each bill in quick succession, feeling for the telltale weight and snap of genuine U.S. currency. It had taken several paydays before he asked her, *sotto voce*, for a date, hoping he didn't come across in a way that would prompt her to press an alarm button.

Yvonne could have easily been mistaken for a California beach bimbo. Her sunny looks and the pale lipstick she favored shouted "shallow blonde." But it was her friendly way, and the fact she worked in a bank, a responsible job, that encouraged Neal to look deeper. On their first date he escorted her aboard his aircraft carrier, USS *Ranger*. Neal thought it would be a good way to begin, in familiar surroundings, where he could keep the conversation going with statistics, logistics and history of the ship. She surprised him by showing interest in him and his ship and continuing to ask questions even afterward, ashore, when they shared dinner at the North Island Officer's Club.

"Hey," she said now, raising her voice when he failed to answer, "comin' to bed?"

Neal looked up. "Think I'll stay up a while, have a beer." He could not bear the thought of sliding into bed with her, as though the mere touch of their bodies would reveal his past infidelity.

Yvonne accepted his response silently and stepped into the kitchen, opening the refrigerator. She returned with an opened long-necked Corona and tipped the bottle to her mouth. As long as they'd been together, Yvonne had claimed the first sip of his beers, a habit she had developed as a child with her father's indifferent indulgence, both in her and in his own beer habit.

"Don't stay up late," she said, handing him the sampled bottle and planting a quick kiss on his lips. The T-shirt billowed as she bent, and he glanced at her trim, well-formed breasts, wishing that he could feel his normal lust for his wife.

Neal leaned back another notch in his recliner, stretching his legs, as Yvonne disappeared down the hallway. He let the possibilities of what might happen as a result of this book unfold slowly. The one he seized on, that life would continue as it had been, seemed optimistic. *No*, he thought, taking a sip from the Corona that he'd held warming in his hand, *nothing would remain the same.*

WHEN NEAL CAME HOME from work the next day, he found Yvonne in the kitchen, a pair of martinis carefully measured out on the kitchen island. One apiece before dinner, a limit she had insisted on. Fine with him. He had given in whenever she came up with a new rule for their marriage, thankful that they still had a marriage. She had shown a mellowing, though, once they'd gotten away from the rigid navy environment.

Neal had gotten a civilian job at Defense Dynamics nine months ago and did not miss the navy as he thought he would. He wasn't interested in being on base, though both Point Mugu Naval Air Station and the Port Hueneme Seabee Base were within a few miles of their home in Camarillo. Sometimes his new job with Defense Dynamics, a government contractor, would require on-base meetings, and he'd go without experiencing a whit of nostalgia. He had gotten beyond his emotional need for the structure the navy had brought to his life after a childhood with a struggling mother and bullying brother. The uncertainty of that life was completely supplanted by the unshakable military organization. Neal admitted to himself that, in spite of his membership in the naval brotherhood, he had remained a loner for much of his career. He convinced himself it was far easier, as a spook, to avoid developing deep friendships that would run the risk of inadvertent revelation of government secrets.

"Chicken piccata tonight," Yvonne said, slicing a tomato. He came from behind and kissed her neck. "Were you late tonight because it's proposal time?"

He breathed in the tang of a pair of reamed lemon halves lying on the counter beside the juicer. "Looks like it. Another one of those 'must-win' contracts for the company. Cruise missiles this time. It'll be a big one. Jarrel's showing his nerves." Jarrel Schneider, the Defense Dynamics Camarillo office director, had flown to Hawaii and recruited Neal for his post-retirement job. The widely reported Kimo incident had caught Jarrel's attention. And it doesn't hurt to have an admired navy officer on staff when you're doing business with the navy, especially an officer with all the requisite security clearances.

THE CHICKEN PICCATA AND rice pilaf finished, candles guttering in the slight breeze off the cooling land, Neal turned his chair to the side, crossed his legs and nursed the remaining chardonnay in his glass. He knew where Yvonne stood regarding alcohol, convincing himself that in complying he wasn't caving in, just being cooperative. Besides, he had come to appreciate the way moderation had made him feel in the morning. He closed his eyes over the grittiness of a long day and lost himself in music as the CD player whispered softly with a Rachmaninoff piano concerto.

"Neal?" Yvonne said in a quiet but unmistakable tone, a signal that she had chosen her time to speak words of importance. He looked up. Candlelight played on her features, the glow peeking past the open-neck blouse, warming the visible curve and cleavage of her breasts. "How do you know Angela Vance?"

His poker-face intelligence officer training failed him now. He drew a deep breath as he ran possible responses through his mind. His heart surged into high gear. Neal raised the wine glass, purchasing time, but his lips had fused together—glued, mouth dry. He was instantly aware of how he looked to Yvonne, how like a criminal he felt. How stupid he'd been to leave the book out.

Yvonne filled his silence. "I found her book in the den. *To Neal Olen, _more_ love and kisses from a hero worshipper.*" She locked him in her gaze, challenging. "*More* love and kisses?"

Nailed. He drew a breath. "It was when we were separated. I met her in a bar. Weekend fling. That's all." He spoke in a dulled voice.

Yvonne leaned forward, elbows planted on the tablecloth, face hard. "You seeing her now?"

"No."

"Don't make me pry it out of you, Neal." The intensity in her voice deepened. "My first impulse was to skip the piccata and use the skillet on your skull. But I'm too fucking civilized."

Truth might save the marriage from a four-year-old screwing, Neal thought. Maybe he had left the book out on purpose—some of that psychological shit about wanting to be caught. "I went to see her yesterday at the Borders in Thousand

Oaks. Met her in the bar next door afterward to talk. Don't worry—she came in with a pair of armed rent-a-cops, and there was nothing pleasant about it. The only interest I have in her is what she might have said in the book about—"

"Had you considered just *reading* the goddamned book? Why did you have to *see* her?"

"More to it than just the book. I had to know what else she might be planning." Now he faced her squarely. "There was a TV interview a couple weeks ago. She made it pretty clear that the book was more than a novel—that it had real people in it. She even talked about a 'navy hero.'. . . ."

A moment's silence. Neal stared at a candle flame, then looked at his wife. Her face had lost some of its granite.

"She wrote about you?" Yvonne's voice came slowly. Her eyes filled.

"Chapter six," he said.

CHAPTER THREE

Just inside the front door of Defense Dynamics, Neal nearly collided with Jarrel Schneider, florid-faced and paunchy, looking to be in need of sleep. It was 7:45 A.M. and Schneider was moving down the hallway at close to a run. Without slowing his pace he launched an order. "Neal, get your coffee, meet me in the puka, ten minutes." Jarrel slapped a fat hand against the men's room door and gave a shove.

The puka—Hawaiian for "hole." The Pacific navy had unofficially adopted the term for the high-security enclosures where top-level classified material was stored. The weapon system development contracts Defense Dynamics had with the Naval Surface Warfare Center at Port Hueneme and the Pacific Missile Test Center at Point Mugu demanded a puka with armed guard.

"Good morning, sir." The guard, a retired navy master-at-arms, examined Neal's badge and handed him a pen to sign in on the clipboard. Another cipher lock and retinal scan a few feet beyond the guard post allowed Neal entry to the top-secret puka. It was like a castle keep, a box within a box able to withstand infiltration, but vulnerable to trusted personnel harboring evil intent—the John Walkers and Aldridge Ameses of the world. Neal was familiar with security routines, the mainstay of his career in the navy's intelligence community. He understood the proper handling of the nation's most secret information and was acutely aware of the consequences for a breach of security—prison, and the possibility of a death sentence during wartime.

Far from the Hollywood version of a top-secret room, the puka's interior was unremarkable, just another windowless office with desks and locking file cabinets, computers on the desks that never left the puka with an intact hard drive. These machines were without links to anything outside the puka. Computer hackers had proven far too successful in their ability to infiltrate supposedly foolproof government secure systems. The room smelled of stale coffee, and there were a few Styrofoam cups on the floor. No janitors had clearances to enter the puka, and Defense Dynamics employees disdained cleanup.

Neal mused that this retirement job was the only positive outcome of his sudden heroic renown when he had saved Kimo Puhoi in 1998. When retired Rear Admiral Jarrel Schneider had tracked Neal down in Hawaii, he'd begun his pitch immediately. "I gotta tell you the truth here, Commander. We like everything we know about you, but what is particularly attractive is that your clearances can be immediately transferred over from the navy. That carries major weight with the company."

Avoiding the expense and time involved in an FBI background check and the convoluted clearance process that had been set up following revelations of espionage at the Los Alamos National Laboratory made it worthwhile for Defense Dynamics to give Neal a $20,000 signing bonus on a three-year contract. Neal would have accepted the position even without the bonus. His quiet demeanor and outward lack of enthusiasm, carefully cultivated over years in the spook game, covered his feeling of elation, made him hesitate. Jarrel Schneider responded with extra relocation money and a partial down payment offer on a house in California.

"Yeah, and we'll pick up the plane and hotel—so you all can check out the Defense Dynamics facility and see about a house. I figure you'd like one of the new places in Spanish Hills above Camarillo," Jarrel had said. Neal would be the Defense Dynamics director of government business development, which meant scouring upcoming contract solicitation notices and developing proposals for highly classified military engineering projects.

The lock clicked behind Neal, dragging him back to the present. Jarrel pushed into the puka and motioned Neal over to an empty desk and chairs. "They're goin' directly to the Block 4 model cruise missile," he said, grinning, passing a hand through his thinning hair and over a perpetually damp forehead. This morning Jarrel appeared bloated, needing to summon extra effort to stand or move.

"You sure? I thought it was supposed to be Block 3 model Tomahawk Multi-Mission Missile with some upgrades." Neal had immersed himself in the latest materials on the current Tomahawk Missile configuration data.

"Dumped it. Going straight to the next model since so much of the ship and sub-launched ordnance is scrap iron in downtown Belgrade. In any case it means a lot more business for us, assuming you put together a shit-hot proposal." The boss wiped his brow with a well-used wad of tissue produced from his jacket pocket.

"Global Positioning System," Jarrel continued. "Getting rid of the old terrain avoidance gear, replacing it with GPS.

About time national defense caught up with backpackers—fucking Sierra Club has better navigation than a Tomahawk." He paused, smiling at his own observation. "Nothing says prosperity like a good little war in Yugoslavia," he said, satisfaction radiating from his pink face.

Neal allowed himself a smile at the news. It would mean job security for him if he could score a win. Such a contract would run for a minimum of five years. Neal's first task would be to comb hundreds of pages of contract requirements. Meanwhile, once the specifics were known, work on the proposal itself would surge. Long days and short tempers would be the rule.

WHEN NEAL CAME HOME that night, he found an envelope bearing the return address CHIEF OF NAVAL PERSONNEL RETIREMENT SECTION, similar to a number of such official correspondences Neal had received over the past nine months, on his desk. It could just be routine paperwork from the navy that came with his changed status from active duty to fleet reserve—not really retired, part of the "inactive reserve force," in military parlance. Yvonne had left it for him with the daily flood of junk mail.

Neal set the navy envelope to the side. He'd deal with the other mail first, pay the mortgage company, soft water service, trash. . . . As he signed the checks and tore them loose at the perforations, his eyes returned to the envelope. A sick feeling developed in his guts. He pushed the unfinished stack of bills aside and reached for this one piece of mail. He turned it over in his hands before picking up the opener to slit the flap.

The letter began with a reference to a Uniform Code of Military Justice Article 32 investigation, the armed forces' somewhat informal version of a grand jury proceeding. It ordered Neal to report to Naval Base San Diego for the hearing. The second sheet carried the charge—violation of UCMJ Article 134, Adultery.

Specification: In that Neal Edward Olen, Commander, U.S. Navy, while on active duty assignment to USS Constellation CV-64, while a married man, on or about October 1995, did wrongfully have sexual intercourse with Angela Vance, a married woman not his wife.

Neal closed the den door and read the letter again. There was also a part about a charge under Article 133, Conduct Unbecoming an Officer and Gentleman, pending further investigation. "Conduct unbecoming," a charge that could be tacked onto any crime at all, bad manners to murder. No question in Neal's mind about this charge, though. Adultery was pretty damned unbecoming, officer or not. No doubt it was listed as pending because they were digging around for more dirt, more unbecoming stuff. His heartbeat rose in his chest and the jazz coming from the CD player made no impression on his brain. The smell of dinner cooking disappeared as his full focus sharpened on the words. He read it again, looking for something that would undo it all. Something to keep him out of the meat grinder of military justice.

Someone's practical joke, maybe. Why would the navy bother with such a common and minor breech? And why now?

No, not a joke; he dismissed the thought. He examined the envelope, turning it over. Genuine postmark—Millington, Tennessee, where the Navy Military Personnel Command had moved from Washington, D.C. . . .

Then he knew. Washington! January '99. State of the Union speech. The reason for this accusation now. Clearly, this was going to be payback for embarrassing the navy before the whole country—for allowing Angela Vance to reveal a hero's clay feet.

He gripped the chair arms until his muscles ached. How could he have forgotten the discomfort of attention at the bidding of Admiral Ellison who had, immediately following the rescue, called Neal before a press conference and pinned the Navy and Marine Corps Medal on him—recognition of selfless heroism for saving a drowning child. The media attention that followed, the personal appearances at high schools to recruit local teenagers into navy enlistment. He remembered, as someone who had shunned attention both personally and professionally, how uncomfortable and exposed he had felt on that October day. And then he was summoned the following January to Washington. He had sat at attention, listening as best he could, while the president of the United States, speaking in his competent, metered way, laid out his plan for the nation before the packed House chamber. Neal sat in the gallery front row overlooking the main floor, just back of the rail, Yvonne in the row directly behind him. She had had no reluctance when that invitation—that obligation—had come to Neal in the form of additional duty travel orders and a pair of airline tickets. The strong pride he had felt at the outset, being awarded the Navy and Marine Corps Medal, had been tempered by his resentment at a sudden change of jobs. Now he was a spokesman for the entire navy, charged with building goodwill. All Neal really wanted was the work he'd been trained for, analyzing intelligence, assessing who the next enemy might be, playing war games on the admiral's staff.

Yvonne had confided to Neal that to her that night wasn't about his embarrassed tedium telling the Kimo story again and again. Nor was it pitching the U.S. Navy as a career when almost anything looked better to a kid in baggy pants. They were at the U.S. Capitol, for God's sake! The president addressing the room, the First Lady sitting three seats down from Neal, close enough for spoken greetings. There was also the reception to come afterward, the introductions and congratulations from important people.

"It's the big payoff, Neal, finally," Yvonne had said as they waited earlier in an anteroom off the House chamber. She stood straight beside him, nearly as tall in her heels. "The years of putting up with navy-this and navy-that and me being the good little navy wife. All the hours you worked, sea duty. You can count on me to be a good navy wife for *this* event," she assured him. She leaned close, kissed his cheek and rubbed away the trace of lipstick quickly with her fingers. "It's all right to be happy, darling—relax," she said, her own voice tremulous.

He had smiled stiffly and put an arm around her shoulder. Neal's training and military bearing prevented anything close to relaxation in the presence of his commander in chief, but he did his best.

The grand legislative chamber had quieted when the president finished lauding two other notable citizen guests and spoke again. Neal could feel Yvonne's fingers touching his back. "Commander Neal Olen is my honored guest tonight because in true American fashion he took decisive steps, without thought or consideration for his own life, to save a disabled child from drowning. Commander Olen's selfless heroism is the reason that Kimo Puhoi is alive today.

"Whoever says there are no American heroes anymore has not met these three! Or the hundreds of other everyday heroes who make a difference, who quietly go about their lives until challenged by fate." The president led the thunderous applause as Neal stood at attention, the smile that he had learned to effect for the cameras in Hawaii pasted on his face. But suddenly he realized that at this moment it was genuine.

CHAPTER FOUR

"**D**inner's ready. Were you on the phone?" Yvonne was standing beside him, having entered the den unnoticed. "Thought I heard you talking."

He turned in the chair to face his wife, looking intently at her eyes, her lithe body, wondering how much longer this would be possible. He raised the papers in his hand to the space between them and locked her eyes in his vision. "Recall orders. Navy's recalling me to active duty." He let his face go blank.

Yvonne lifted her apron, gathering it in her hands, wiping her fingers before reaching to take the sheet of paper. She held it up as if to read, but tears brimmed and tracked her face, leaving a mascara trail on each cheek. She cast the letter on the desk. "But you're retired," she said, wariness, defiance, entering her tone. "You're done with all that shit."

Neal shook his head slowly, eyes downcast. Yvonne knew better, knew that he was still subject to military law and recall as long as he drew pay—active duty or retirement. She just didn't want to know.

"The navy's like the Mafia. You can only escape by dying," she said.

"It's a court-martial, in San Diego."

"Don't go. You don't have to go. Tell 'em to go to hell; tell 'em you've got a good job now, you've done your twenty years." Yvonne spoke rapidly as though it would help her claw out of this abyss. "It's that bitch's book, isn't it. *More love and kisses* . . . from the navy!" She lifted the apron to her face, sopping the tears. "Can't . . . they just . . . leave us alone?"

He stood, encircling her shoulders with his arms, his face in her hair. Minutes passed before Yvonne pushed away from his embrace, eyes red, moist.

"What'll you do? What'll *we* do?"

"Get a lawyer," he said, because he had no other answer.

"*NAVY WENCH*—GREAT TITLE." Curtis Rassiter slid his horn-rimmed bifocals up to the bridge of his nose, scooted his chair forward tight to the desk, and opened the envelope Neal had brought to their meeting. The gray-haired lawyer showed more than passing curiosity in the recall order. A plaque on the wall bearing the recognizable Judge Advocate General Corps insignia identified Rassiter as a former navy lawyer, as had the yellow pages ad for his Ventura office. "This ought to be interesting. The book's supposed to be fiction, right? So on that basis there is no case unless the author refutes that it is made up."

"She's pretty much done that. Her idea of sales promotion is to make it known that the book is essentially true," Neal answered. Tightness in his throat raised the pitch of his voice. Attempts to sleep the night before had been futile.

"You're telling me that the adultery charge is true." A beat. "Of course it's true. I've seen her picture." Rassiter chuckled.

"Technically—"

"No 'technically' about it, Commander. You did her or you didn't, while you were married."

"Separated."

"No matter. Until you're divorced you're married. The military doesn't recognize separation as a legal condition— probably not even as a mitigating factor. Don't even try that one. It says in the specification that she is a married woman. Right?"

"Never asked. She never said and I didn't see a wedding band."

"Four years ago, you said?"

Neal nodded.

"Still within the statute of limitations." Rassiter opened a copy of the *Manual for Courts-Martial*. "I'm curious about the pending charge on conduct unbecoming. Could be anything from reading someone else's mail or cheating on a test to failing to support your family. And in between we find drunk and disorderly and defamatory language and every possible act, *enumerated or not*, that could dishonor an officer. It's usually automatic in adultery cases. Something's missing if they're holding off on drawing up the specification until the Article 32 investigation. That, along with the 'married woman' thing, tells me there's another angle. And there's no doubt lots of pressure from high up to get the proceedings under way."

Neal drew a slow breath. "What kind of chance do I have to beat this?"

"No way to know without more information." Rassiter thumbed a few pages of the *Manual for Courts-Martial*, reading briefly, then flipped the volume shut. "I'd love to take this case, but I can't be gone from here that long. Anyway, I'd have to tack a per diem on to your bill in San Diego.

You'd be better off with someone down there." He rummaged in a drawer, then handed Neal a business card. "I recommend her. Admits to being a vicious bitch, and she beat me in military court more than once. She's an ex-JAG with a hard-on for the navy, 'specially sex cases."

"Hard-on?"

Rassiter laughed. "You'll understand when you meet her in San Diego. Navy legal services will appoint a junior JAG officer as your defense for free, but make sure she's your lead attack dog. She's well worth the money. If anyone can save your ass, it'll be her."

Rassiter stood and extended a hand. "Good luck, Commander."

Neal left the lawyer's office with a greater understanding of what he faced but no more confidence that he could beat it. He'd have to track down Angela Vance regardless, find out what else there might be awaiting him, what else she might have done to destroy his life.

He drew the card Rassiter had given him from his pocket: LETHAJOY BELTOWER, ESQUIRE, it said, UCMJ DEFENSE.

NEAL DROVE HIS MIATA into the hills behind Ventura. Stopping at a small park above the city government buildings, he could see the century-old wooden pier jutting into the surf. Street lights below were coming on as the sun made its dip. He leaned on the steering wheel, letting his eyes go out of focus, allowing the shimmering images to soften and confuse. *Midforties*, he thought, *and still haunted by childhood.* The same helpless, disconnected feeling had returned. He had successfully—but now, clearly, only temporarily—pushed it away, projecting confidence that he hadn't always felt during his navy career. It was the uniform, the display of rank, that had protected him.

It was after he was back on the ferry's deck with Kimo that memories of his own childhood in Carson City had come rushing back. He had watched the child helpless, struggling, unable to control himself or his surroundings. Neal had pushed the memories aside, but he could not forget the betrayal he had endured at the hands of his brother, the fear of retribution. And it was happening again.

Dad had stormed out of their half of the flat-roofed Carson City house, slamming the front door with a concussive thump, the screen door following with a screech of the coil spring, a slap of wood, and bellowing from the man next door to *shut the fuck up—it's midnight*. Chester Olen had made his noisy departure following a particularly loud battle with the boys' mother, Trudy. Rich and Neal lay awake in their shared room listening to her sobs through the wall. Neither dared move, fearing their father would return still in a rage or their mother would finish the fight using them as surrogates, so they feigned sleep until her crying ceased.

Rich, by three years the elder brother, spoke with soft intensity: "I ought to kill that son of a bitch. He better stay away." At fourteen Rich could sound not only like he meant it but like he could do it. He had memories that reached back to before Dad had succumbed to the drugs and the gambling, while he still paid the bills and had been fun, before Mom had to haul drinks in a seedy casino for minimum wage and tips.

Back in the Miata above the city, Neal pushed the past aside, telling himself he had to concentrate on the present, on salvaging what he could of his present life. But he had been in the navy too long to believe that he would be facing anything less than the full power of its legal system.

JARREL SCHNEIDER STOOD with effort, pushing the chair back on its wheels, and turned to the windows that formed the corner of his Defense Dynamics office. Neal recrossed his legs, attempting calm after yesterday's bad news from Rassiter. He expected instead that the tense atmosphere in the office was about to ignite. Just outside the window an American flag snapped in the stiff breeze, the hoisting lanyards rhythmically striking the pole in a metallic tattoo. He guessed that the air must have been like this in the White House just before Nixon resigned—everyone sweating, not knowing where to look, how to sit, who to point at. The difference here was that Neal had no one to point to, even if that had been his game.

"The timing couldn't be worse, Neal. How'd you suggest we handle this cruise missile proposal without you? You can't take classified work to San Diego." Jarrel displayed his level of concern by forgoing his usual bluster.

Neal shifted in the chair that Jarrel had once confided to him was chosen purposely for its lack of comfort—a wooden crosspiece under a thin cushion. The butt-bruising chair was to discourage campers, he had said. Keep people awake when I'm talking.

"We've got cleared engineers, Jarrel—people who'd be working on the missile contract. They could be shifted temporarily to the proposal team," Neal said.

"That's the whole reason I hired you. You don't think like an engineer—don't write like an engineer. I tried using 'em before. Got so bogged down arguing over minutia we had to get Vicki out from Arlington to take over." Jarrel spoke to the window, his breath clouding a circle on the plate glass.

"Maybe Vicki—"

"Laid off. There's nothing but a skeleton crew left at headquarters. We've got no proposal talent left there. That's what we get for trying to spread ourselves around—a chance to fuck up in new and exciting ways."

"Maybe I can clear this thing up in San Diego and be back in time to manage the proposal," Neal said, not seriously believing that a "maybe" would be an option or that anything navy would go quickly.

"When do you have to report?" Jarrel asked, turning to face his employee.

"Two weeks. I'll get as much done as I can with the information we've got 'til then."

"Goddamn it, Neal, you know that won't amount to shit. I can't afford false starts. I have to find someone quick, a freelancer who can honcho it from the beginning, whenever it hits—keep some continuity." Jarrel cast his glance down at his desk, paused, then raised his eyes to Neal. "Find a replacement," he said.

There was nothing to say—not now, with Jarrel riding the carefully controlled edge of an explosion. Neal went to his own office, flipped through the Rolodex and began calling likely candidates for his job.

"SORRY, SIR, YOU ARE going to have to leave the area immediately." The security guard walked quickly from his station at the door of the top-secret puka, blocking Neal's way. "Your clearance has been suspended, sir. I'm just waiting for the facility security officer to come change combinations." His right hand dropped, his thumb resting lightly on the grip of his holstered 9-millimeter Glock. "Now, sir." No mistaking the sentry's meaning.

"Shit," Neal said as he turned to leave the classified enclosure feeling as though the guard had used the pistol to put a slug in his gut. The shock of having his clearances pulled—maybe permanently—was more than a simple administrative function; it felt like both an insult and a personal attack. Neal suddenly was no longer to be trusted with his nation's sensitive information, materials he had conscientiously, zealously protected for twenty years. It was also a message that the navy legal system had shifted into high gear. Without access to classified material, his career with Defense Dynamics or any other defense contractor was effectively over. He knew well that had he been making the decision about someone else, he would have pulled clearances in an instant. No such thing as waiting for due process with national security at stake. A suspicion was enough, had to be enough. A person facing felony charges might flee to a foreign country, taking a little classified material along— a little gift to a willing host, a little life insurance. A little treason.

Outside the secret workroom door, in the Defense Dynamics basement passageway, Wayne Corby, the company's facility security officer, approached carrying a small tool kit he used for changing safe combinations and cipher locks.

"I guess the guard gave you the word," Wayne said softly. "Sorry. I wanted to tell you myself in private, but I had to take care of the combos first. You understand. The cancellation notice from Defense Security Service was in my e-mail this morning. Coded urgent."

Neal stood mute, understanding perfectly, not knowing where to look.

Wayne touched Neal's sleeve. "Have to take your badge, partner. Building keys too."

Neal worked the keys off the ring, leaving only his house and car keys, then pulled the ID tag chain over his head and held it out. Wayne took the keys and plastic identification badge bearing the colored stripes signifying Neal's clearance level.

Wayne Corby turned to the cipher lock on the secret room door, then glanced at Neal. "I'll be a while. See you after lunch. I'll give you your debriefing, sign some paperwork then. OK, Neal?" Wayne's gentle but unmistakable cue was for Neal to leave.

"BRING ME ANYTHING YOU'RE working on that you can still get to." Jarrel Schneider had set about to effect damage control. Jarrel would have to take over Neal's job, at least for the present. The old admiral went about the task with an efficiency born of his thirty-year military background.

"You remember you signed a three-year contract, Neal—it hasn't been a year yet. I won't bother about that now, but since you can't perform, you're not only in breach but you've put the company in extremis. I'll ask Arlington to hold off doing anything about recovering the bonus and the house money until we know what your status will be with the navy. You get your clearances reinstated and maybe we can use you again, though I can't promise. If we hire new people to replace you, we can't just bounce 'em after a few months. Lawyers will have to work out some kind of settlement. Sorry, Neal, I've got no choice." Jarrel dragged the tissue wad from his pocket and mopped his forehead, then reached for the telephone, turning his attention away from Neal.

YVONNE MET NEAL AT the kitchen door, a frightened, angry fire in her eyes. "God, Neal, reporters already started calling. I told them you were at work. One of them said he'd tried Defense Dynamics and that you weren't there. Where've you been all day?"

"Driving . . . thinking."

"Don't leave out drinking! I can smell it." Yvonne stood in the kitchen door frame, her feet planted. "You didn't quit your job, did you?"

"I didn't have to quit," he said. "The government suspended my clearance. I'm worthless to Defense Dynamics now. Jarrel said I was in breach of the employment contract. Probably have to give back the bonus money, down payment—"

Her slap caught them both unaware, stinging his cheek, leaving his earlobe bleeding where a fingernail had struck. Yvonne raised a hand to her mouth. She drew a sharp breath. Neither of them had ever hit the other.

The pain came almost as a relief to Neal. If only it could be an equitable trade for the load of grief he had brought home with him to Yvonne.

"Come on, goddamnit, might as well give it all to me," Yvonne said, recovering some of her ire, the edge of her voice like a sword. "Get it over with. What's that piece of ass going to cost? Where are we going to live?"

He extended a hand toward her but let it drop when he saw she could not respond, that tears now overflowed her eyes. "Can we sit?" he asked, feeling like a stranger in his home.

"Do we still own the furniture?" she asked, her voice softening in tone but still carrying an edge of hurt and sarcasm. Yvonne walked past the couch where he sat, her limp evident, as it usually was when she was tired. She took the recliner, sitting forward on the edge of the cushion, elbows on knees, eyes on him.

"It gets worse," Neal said. "Rassiter, the lawyer, said conviction on the adultery charge could be a year in prison and loss of retirement pay—same for conduct unbecoming."

"How can they do that? They'd wipe us out financially, and we'd be in debt to Defense Dynamics—no way to pay it off." Yvonne's speech came rapidly. "Then what? After prison, they wouldn't give back your clearances, would they? I can teach, but it would take everything I earned just to live. Christ, Neal."

In the silence that developed Yvonne glanced around the Spanish Hills house as though it would disappear the next instant. Cathedral ceilings, massive fireplace, polished oak floors, even a whirlpool in the bathroom. It was unlike anything she'd had before.

"There's the life insurance . . . ," Neal said quietly, head down, studying his shoes.

"No!" Yvonne said, stiffening.

"It would bring a half million and it's way past the two-year clause."

Yvonne crossed the space to her husband in an instant, wrapping him in an angry embrace, her hands finding purchase on his shoulders, in his hair.

Neal could not respond to his wife's fear and sat limp in her arms. This was not him; this had to be a movie, happening to someone else. Suicide had never seriously crossed his mind before today. It had come to him while sitting at a bar for the afternoon, waiting to go home at Defense Dynamics' quitting time, as if the pretense of normalcy could change the facts. But now it looked more like an answer as the vise of defeat closed on his life, squeezing dry all that he and Yvonne had worked for. It would save on the embarrassment of a navy show trial for him, for her. One shot to the brain and he'd be a one-day headline. The media would lose interest when they couldn't pester him. The story would be over for Yvonne and might redeem a piece of his honor. Why not? It had worked for Admiral Boorda, the chief of naval operations who had pressed a pistol to his heart in 1996. That was over a scrap of metal, a single award he may not have been entitled to wear amid his chest full of ribbons.

She held his head to her breast and rocked gently while tears fell on his hair.

"Costa Rica," Yvonne said after a time. "Why not run off to Costa Rica? Start over."

They had discussed it once in Hawaii, before the Defense Dynamics offer had come. They could live well there on his navy retirement check alone. They had ordered a book and video, explored the foreign community there, what they could expect from San José. But now there might not be a retirement check or any other way to earn a Yankee dollar.

THE THREE VODKA MARTINIS Neal had drunk over Yvonne's silent protest had not given him sudden courage. They hadn't led him to seek out the revolver on the top shelf of the closet. Instead, he had dropped off into a troubled sleep.

After maybe an hour Neal stirred, opened his eyes briefly as he tried to roll away from a twist of blanket. He saw Yvonne watching him, or perhaps watching over him. He flopped his arm limply across the covers and felt her take his hand. His mind drifted to images of prison, of the navy's Correctional Custody Unit in San Diego where he'd once gone to see one of his subordinates doing a three-month term for drug possession. Rather than individual cells, inmates were kept in what could only be called large cages, holding twenty or more. And unlike the boisterous penitentiaries Neal had seen in movies, military prison inmates were kept in strictly enforced silence. Shouted orders of the marine guards were the only sounds that rose above a quiet rustle and murmur.

When Neal had been there, he witnessed prisoners individually pulled from the cages for rule infractions. They were made to brace against the wall at stiff attention or forced to exercise to exhaustion while a pair of guards hurled invective at them. And that was when visitors were present. Stories with stark details of greater physical and mental abuse for uncooperative sorts were common. Officers—former officers—were rumored to be given particularly hard treatment by both guards and other inmates.

The navy's Portsmouth prison was closed, so he'd probably land in Fort Leavenworth or one of the federal penitentiaries.

YVONNE FOUND HIM IN the den the next morning facing the computer, staring at the screen.

"You're not still thinking about committing—about the insurance, are you? Just tell me how I can help. I'm your wife. And I'm so sorry that I hit you."

"I'm OK now."

"How long you been up?"

"Around five," he said, raising an arm to cradle her waist.

"What're you doing?" she asked, glancing at the computer screen.

"Looking for an address, phone number, anything on Angela. I've got to talk to her, find out what all she's said, what, if anything, she's told the navy."

"Does this mean you've forgotten about the insurance?"

He looked up into her face, her fine, soft skin creased from sleeping on wrinkled bedding. It only made her more beautiful and intriguing. "It seemed like the only answer when everything came down on me yesterday—losing my clearance, my job, on top of those recall orders. It felt like I was already dead. But that's not me, Yvonne." He tightened his arm around her waist, allowing himself a tiny smile. "I woke up this morning remembering something Rassiter had said—the book is fiction. The whole thing hangs entirely on what Angela says is true and what isn't. Maybe if she understands the effect. . . . Besides, if I killed myself over this, she'd love it. Probably drive her book to the top of the best-sellers—the bump she's been looking for. I'm not going to do her the favor."

"I'll get a job," Yvonne announced, "at least until we can get through this. Been thinking about going back to teaching anyway."

He resisted the impulse to wave off her offer because he had no idea of when or whether they might get past this thing. Their savings didn't amount to that much—fifty, sixty thousand. There were also the savings bonds Neal had been collecting from the time he'd joined the navy. They'd probably need them for the legal bills. It made sense for Yvonne to apply at the school district, get in as a substitute where she could, wait for full-time. California needed more elementary school teachers with the recent class-size reduction legislation.

"We might have to move into something smaller," Neal said. "I wonder how much this place might have appreciated in nine months."

Yvonne leaned down, gave him a quick kiss. "Brush your teeth, Romeo. I'll put on some coffee."

CHAPTER FIVE

"Curtis Rassiter said you might call." Lethajoy Beltower's voice came through the receiver smooth, strong, a hint of Boston in the overtones. "He said that you got crosswise with the navy and they're trying to make an adultery charge stick. When'll you be here?"

"I'm supposed to report next Monday. I could drive down earlier if there would be any point to it—assuming I can get past the media. Why are they so interested in this?"

"Come on, Commander, it's got everything—sex, celebrity, heroism, revenge. And, you know, the golden idol with a fatal flaw. Add some courtroom drama and you got *Perry Mason* meets *Masterpiece Theater*." A pause. "I'm not making fun of your dilemma, but look at it like this and you can see why there's such an interest." Ms. Beltower sounded a bit too chipper, but hers was the only lawyer's name Neal had at the moment.

"I guess . . ."

"In the meantime, don't make any statements to the press. Forget the 'no comment' stuff; it only makes you look guilty, like you're hiding something, like a politician." Neal heard the sound of pages rustling. "How 'bout we meet Friday, 9 A.M. See whether we have a case. Meantime I'll do some snooping. I expect the Article 32 investigation will be scheduled pretty quick. I can't imagine they'd want to delay show time."

The instant Neal lowered the receiver to its cradle it rang, startling him into raising it automatically, instead of letting it go to the machine. "Yes?"

"Neal, Wayne Corby. Can you come to the office right away?" The Defense Dynamics facility security officer sounded concerned, somber.

"You forget I'm persona non grata?" Neal said.

"Listen, Jarrel's dead—heart attack, stroke, don't know. . . ."

Neal could say nothing for the moment, guilty thoughts racing through his mind. *Perhaps the added pressure on Jarrel, from me leaving.* "When did it. . . ."

"Don't know for sure, Neal," Wayne said, sounding, in an odd way, slightly irritated. "We found him in the puka this morning. Could have been there all night."

"Damn. How's Martha taking it?"

"She knew he had health problems, of course. But after thirty-seven years of marriage. . . . She's pretty much in shock. But listen, the boss is on a plane from Arlington. He wants to see you. Nobody else knows as much as you do about the proposal. You were the last one to discuss it with Jarrel, as far as we can tell."

"But my clearances . . ."

"That only means that we can't tell *you* anything. We need a brain dump—everything you know, Neal. The company's depending on you."

Neal would have told Wayne to shove it, if there weren't the slimmest ray of hope that one day, when all this navy mess was cleared up, Defense Dynamics would rehire him.

That, plus the thousands of dollars in unearned bonus Neal owed the company, argued against getting too pissy about it. Meantime, he decided, nothing to do but eat dirt, give them what they want. Besides, there was little else constructive he could do before driving to San Diego Thursday night for the Friday morning meeting with Lethajoy Beltower.

YVONNE HAD RESPONDED WITH concern when he told her about Jarrel's death. "So sudden," she said. "Martha must be devastated. She's been trying to get Jarrel to slow down for years." When Neal left her, she kissed him slowly, carefully, as though he, too, were fragile.

"I'll call Martha," she said as he stepped into the garage.

The hours-long questioning and Neal's recitation of the salient points of his Tomahawk Multi-Mission Missile research—necessary for understanding how the GPS guidance might be worked in as an upgrade—lasted into the night. Wayne ordered in pizza and wore a sour face. The nonstop talk and fast food left a bitter taste at the back of Neal's mouth and he could feel his eyes drying up in the over-air-conditioned space. During toilet breaks Neal had Wayne as an escort. Further humiliation under the company's security procedures.

"Making sure I don't grab some company toilet paper, Wayne?" Neal had commented wearily as Wayne stood beside him at the urinals.

"Shut the fuck up, Neal," Wayne said, using a sarcastic, please-pass-the-sugar tone. "This company's on the verge of rolling over, going tits up. All of us'll be out looking for work. Jarrel killed himself trying to carry *your* load."

Neal zippered his fly and stepped back a pace, cheeks tingling with anger. "What are you accusing me of, Wayne?

You looking for someone to pin this on? Use your head. Jarrel had a heart condition and was overweight. I'm done here." Neal left Wayne Corby standing in the men's room.

As HE TURNED THE Miata into his driveway, a powerful light came on, blinding him. He stomped the brake, skidding before he came to a stop. A face appeared at the window, a microphone thrust into the car. He batted it away.

"Is the story in the book true, Commander? *Did* you sleep with Angela Vance?"

The microphone and an arm pushed back into the car. Neal quickly rolled up the window, trapping the hand.

"Ow, goddamnit!" the faceless voice blurted.

He reversed the window and the questioner's hand pulled clear, the cordless microphone falling into his lap as Neal idled the car forward. The cameraman sidestepped, the video camera and floodlight wavering. Neal stopped the Miata and leaned out the window. Several more flood lights came on as cameramen and reporters surged toward him. He threw the microphone to the driveway and watched the first cameraman clutch at his earphones with both hands, the camera falling from his shoulder to the pavement.

"Get off my property now," Neal hissed, and another light centered on him, panning over from the man who had lost his microphone and who now stood bent slightly forward, rubbing his wrist. Neal turned from the floodlight bathing his face, squinting, a ghost image dancing in his brilliance-blasted retinas. He accelerated up the driveway as the three-car garage door crawled upward on its tracks.

Inside the garage with the door down, Neal sat breathing fast, heart beating a rapid cadence. *How the fuck am I going to ignore that?* he asked himself, remembering Lethajoy Beltower's admonition. The kitchen door opened, letting a shaft of light into the garage. "Come in, Neal, come in. They're showing you on television—what just happened. They had it live during the news." Yvonne pulled the car door open. "I wish you hadn't done that. The bastards are already crucifying you. They've been camped out on the street this afternoon since about six."

He swung his legs out of the car and stood, uncertainly, steadying himself with a hand on the hood of Yvonne's Honda Accord. "Assault, trespassing, restricting my movements . . ." all he could remember from his college law class. "Bastards are still out there. Oughta call the cops." Yvonne threw her arms around him, holding tightly for a moment.

They were still showing the fifteen-second tape on the 11 o'clock news, but the frequency of encores had slowed. It would be sure to pick up with the next news cycle on the LA morning shows. Past midnight, the video trucks with their satellite link equipment finally pulled away. Neal and Yvonne collapsed into bed and slept in exhaustion.

"YOU CAN REACH ME at the Wickford Hotel in Chicago. I'll be here two days." Angela Vance left the hotel number on the answering machine. The night before, with the media camped outside, Neal had turned off the telephone ringer. With the volume turned to zero, the only indication of an incoming call was a series of whirs and clicks from the vintage answering machine. The same machine had earlier held the evidence of the media flurry over the Kimo rescue in Hawaii.

Yvonne had ended Neal's frustration in trying to find Angela's number on the Internet, suggesting that it would be unlisted anyway. She had left a message with Angela's publisher. Her gently pointing out Neal's *intelligence failure* was the first friendly gibe Yvonne had taken at him since she had seen Angela's handwritten message to him on the flyleaf of *Navy Wench*.

Yvonne left him alone in the den with his morning cup of coffee, closing the door quietly on her way out while he dialed the Chicago number. The Wickford Hotel front desk put him through to Angela's room.

"Neal, I saw what happened with the reporter. I don't blame you. They can be *so* rude but ya gotta love 'em."

"I need to know what you told the navy," he said slowly, clearly, so there would be no mistaking the gravity of his words. "They're putting me on trial for what you've been saying. I could go to prison, lose my retirement, my home . . . everything. Already lost my job over it."

There was a pause before Angela answered. "God, I'm sorry about that, Neal. I had no idea. I never meant to make trouble for you, but isn't it just like 'em? It illustrates the whole point of *Navy Wench* beautifully, Neal. How they treat people. Anal chickenshits."

"What did you tell the navy investigator?"

"I didn't *tell 'em* anything. Haven't seen anyone. Been on this damn book tour for a month. Maybe they can't find me. Maybe they don't particularly give a shit."

"They give a shit, all right, Angela. You've rubbed their faces in it just when they were starting to rebuild credibility. And now I'm a big goddamned embarrassment." He drew a breath to steady his nerves, to avoid lashing out at her. "What will you testify to at the court-martial?"

"I'll have to send my regrets. Previous plans and all. So you've got nothing to worry about from me."

"You can't send regrets to a federal subpoena," Neal said flatly.

THE WOMAN STOOD NEAR the unoccupied receptionist's desk thumbing through a stack of mail. She looked to be in her midthirties and was wearing black shorts, a black-and-white striped jersey, and cleats covered in mud and grass. She glanced up as Neal entered the attorney's office, which was on the third floor of a nondescript building in a San Diego industrial area. "Commander Olen?" she asked, dropping the stack of envelopes on the desk, advancing, hand outstretched. "Lethajoy Beltower."

"Pleased to meet you, Ms. Beltower." Neal managed to return the handshake without betraying his surprise that this was the lawyer he was counting on to get him out of this mess. *Dress-down Friday?*

"First names, OK? I find that it's easier."

Why be surprised, he told himself. *In California no one has a last name anymore.* "Sure," Neal said.

"Please pardon the sweat. I didn't have a chance to shower and get here on time. I don't usually meet clients in soccer gear. We've got a Friday morning league. We ran long today. Just a bunch of lawyers kicking each other's shins. Good practice for the courtroom." She turned, leading the way to the inner office, speaking rapidly. "Can I get you anything, Neal? Juice, soft drink, bran muffin?"

He declined and sat in the chair that Lethajoy Beltower, Esquire, had indicated. She rounded her desk, a construction of heavily lacquered wooden ship hatch covers, and dropped into the swivel chair. She immediately opened a folder containing a few sheets and pulled a legal pad toward her. The lawyer's hair was cut severely short. She was compact at just over five feet. Her features were fine, but her eyebrows sprouted uncontrolled, unplucked. Neal saw no trace of makeup.

"I got the legal center on base to fax over the charge sheet and the recall letter by telling them I represented you—technically a falsehood, but it gives us a jump on things. I'm intrigued by the allegations." She folded her hands. "First, though, before I get all excited about this, we need to determine whether you want to retain my services. What I can tell you is that I'm aggressive and I'm smart. I win 90 percent of my cases. I've been a navy JAG officer so I know the game and a lot of the players." She leaned forward, pausing, holding eye contact. "I was forced to resign my commission five years ago."

"Mr. Rassiter mentioned—"

"I know—my 'hard-on' for the navy. Thinks it's funny." Her face clouded for an instant, eyebrows dipping like a caterpillar mating dance. "OK, we'll get it out of the way. Under other circumstances I wouldn't mention this. I need to know where you stand, because if you have any objections, any at all, we can quit right now." She took a second to survey Neal's expression. "I left the navy because I was accused of being a lesbian. It destroyed my effectiveness, they said. I got pressured to resign for the good of the service." She let her pronouncement sink in. "You can understand how it gives me pure pleasure to take cases like yours *for the good of the service*." Ms. Beltower folded her hands on the desk, watching Neal for reaction.

Neal kept a poker face, true to his intelligence training. He waited for her to continue.

"In case you're wondering," she said finally, "the accusation was correct. Does it matter to you?" She locked Neal in her gaze.

Neal allowed himself a half smile. "Mr. Rassiter also said if anyone could save my ass, you can. At the moment that's all that really matters."

"Well, Neal, you want your ass saved by an ex-navy, cashiered, vicious bitch lesbian with a hard-on?"

"It would make my wife happy." Neal was thinking about Yvonne's hesitation when he'd told her he needed to go to San Diego alone, that at this stage there was nothing she could do to help.

"I don't *do* client's wives."

"I mean, considering the charges, she won't have to wonder about . . ."

"That's between you and her."

Neal considered what she had said and revisited his thoughts about the continuous military flap over gay service members. He couldn't quite understand the dichotomy of some navy men who'd express their willingness, even jokingly, to roll a gay guy for his money while harboring their own sexual fantasies of two women together. The lesbian mystique, so well employed in the skin magazines, had gained tacit acceptance among navy men as long as it was kept at a distance—as long as it was used for under-the-covers solo entertainment.

Assured that Neal planned to retain her, Lethajoy outlined an opening strategy. It was without enthusiasm that Neal agreed to Lethajoy's weekend assignment to reread *Navy Wench*, in particular, *his* chapter—chapter six.

"Put your emotions aside and read for content," Lethajoy instructed. "Analyze for every point in the story that can be shown to be patently false—even things like street names, restaurants. Any luck and we can quash this thing at the Article 32 investigation. Prove the novel really *is* fiction to the investigating officer, and maybe we can stop a court-martial," Lethajoy said. Pausing, she studied his face for a moment.

She rose and filled her cup with dark coffee from the chrome percolator that stood on a small table near the window. Over her shoulder she said, "It is probably futile trying to prove a novel to be true or false. Not like an autobiography where everything's supposedly true. But you can't even count on that." Neal shifted in the chair, wondering whether he ought to take notes. She carried her coffee mug to the desk. "That's what makes this case interesting. The novel is the wild card that they're using as their probable cause to initiate an investigation, but they can't really rely on it as evidence."

"How is this thing going to run?" Neal gave up the idea of taking notes, counting on the capacity to recall details that he had developed, particularly helpful in his foreign assignments.

"First the pretrial investigation, the military's rough equivalent of a grand jury. It's better than the civilian version in that the accused can participate, ask questions, try to shoot holes in the government's case, a bit of a trial before the trial. Fulfills the need for 'discovery' where both sides can view the other's evidence." She took a sip, made a face and put the cup on the desk.

"The navy likes to assign a Judge Advocate General Corps officer to do the hearing but it could be any officer. Way I see it," she said, "the senior JAGs won't want to risk what I might remember about their own sexual transgressions. Before they figured out I was lesbian, they were all over me wanting dates or a little interlude during the day. Coffee break and a grope.

"The investigating officer makes a recommendation as to whether there is a case, whether charges ought to be referred and sent forward for court-martial. The drawback is that witnesses don't actually have to be there if they aren't locally available. Getting Angela Vance to appear is impossible if she doesn't want to. There's no subpoena power over uncooperative civilians until we get to court-martial—then we can use a big hammer." Lethajoy placed her hands on the desk, leaned forward and lowered her voice as though readying to reveal a confidence. "In our case, for the Article 32 investigation we're probably better off without her anyway unless you know positively how she'll testify, that she will clear you. It will also depend on whether the prosecution has a case without her testimony. Have you got any idea what she might say?"

"She wasn't very forthcoming when I spoke to her on the phone. I wouldn't bet she'd be any friendlier in court—it's all still a joke to her." Neal paused, allowing his gaze to rest on the papers scattered on the lawyer's desk. "What about character witnesses, if I can find any? There must still be someone around who I knew aboard *Constellation*."

"Low priority—don't waste your time. Sure, they could possibly help in mitigating any sentencing, but for the moment it doesn't matter—*Yes, Your Honor, my client is guilty, but he's kind to animals.*

"I expect that since it's an informal proceeding they'll have the pretrial investigation scheduled next week. That's OK—it will give us a chance to assess the situation right away since there isn't much we can pursue until we see their evidence. It's not like a murder or a robbery where you can collect evidence from a crime scene to see which way it points." Lethajoy ran fingers through her hair, revealing an elbow stained with grass and mud.

Neal finally realized the question he'd been wanting to ask her—ask anybody, really. "Why is the navy bothering with this?"

"I frankly don't know for sure," Lethajoy said, "but I can speculate. *Navy Wench* is off limits; the navy can't do a thing to Angela Vance without breaking the law or, at the very least, looking like First Amendment bullies. But they can come after you. There have been cases recently where senior officers have gotten off with a wink and a nod on sex charges while enlisted people got nailed. It looks suspiciously like a double standard—even Congress has taken note. It's become a public relations nightmare at a time when the navy is already having a problem recruiting."

Neal nodded, adding, "I know that ships are deploying undermanned and there's a lot of grumbling from surface warfare officers about their workload, but I still can't see why they want *me*."

Neal's question hung in the air, sounding more and more like whining as it went without answer.

"There's a Washington think tank that's taking a look at the UCMJ," Lethajoy continued. "They appointed a commission of military judges and lawyers to come up with some recommendations for changes, to bring military law into closer alignment with civilian law. Early reports are pretty clear that they are going to recommend that adultery and consensual sodomy be dropped as crimes. Of course it's up to Congress." Lethajoy tapped her pen rapidly on the desk blotter. "I suppose it could look like going after you is a final act of defiance. It wouldn't be the first time the military told Congress to stuff it. Look what happened after 'don't ask, don't tell' went into effect. Gay discharges have increased every year since." She tossed the pen neatly into her IN basket.

"And there's the added bonus that if they nail you, it will help repair the perception of a double standard. That helps recruiting and retention. It shows that even hero officers aren't above military justice."

"Damn." Neal could see how it all fit together—how he could be a useful pawn. Hadn't he been assigned to recruiting duty after the Kimo incident because of the image he presented for the navy? And now he was helping them out again, though unwittingly.

"Here's the cute part." Lethajoy Beltower punctuated her words with a pointed finger. "Since you're retired, they can make the point without losing anyone from the active duty roster. With a conviction you'd lose retainer pay so you're even a cost-effective solution."

"You're serious? . . . Of course you are. Any chance to stop this thing?" Neal asked.

"There's always a chance," Lethajoy said.

◀ ★ ||| CHAPTER SIX

Neal leaned back on the couch in his assigned suite in the Navy Base San Diego Visiting Officers Quarters and opened the back cover of *Navy Wench*. Angela Vance's glamour photo stared back at him from the dust jacket flap. Immediately, anxiety gripped his chest at the thought of reading her damning words, words that to any other man would be a turn-on. He had no choice but to take the assignment Lethajoy had given him.

Navy Wench
Chapter 6

He sat at the bar in the Tortured Tortilla restaurant, somber faced, staring into his margarita. Gillian hadn't seen him in her favorite haunt before tonight. Fresh meat, she thought, and slid onto a barstool one over from him. How long would it take to get him to speak? He didn't look like a player but she'd try the game with him anyway. The scar over one eye made him look dangerous, something that always stirred Gillian's interest. This specimen lacked the predatory look, though. It was more like he'd been tamed first and then cast back into the wilderness—reintroduced to an unfamiliar habitat—like the zoo-hatched California condors. The guy would probably need a refresher course on sex.

Except for the military haircut that made his skull look like a peach, he didn't seem to fit the category of obnoxious dorks who usually hung out in here. The pilots—fighter and attack jocks—who expected women to fall on their backs, knees apart, at the very sight of them. They missed the whole female thing, couldn't see over their egos. Sure, sex was a big part of it, but Gillian would rather have someone cook her a decent meal first—then she'd think about where to put her knees. Gillian guessed that in spite of his rough-looking demeanor, she had found a gentleman this time.

She swung around on the stool, making sure her skirt slipped away from her knee, and locked eyes with her target. "It's OK to talk if you want." She loved his look of surprise.

"Drink?" this one said.

Original, Gillian thought. "Cuba Libre," she answered, giving him the smile. Gillian Libre, she said to herself, feeling the freedom of having a husband off for three months in Pensacola attending a navy school. Ken Lorenz, her mistake of a husband, was a throwback, like some hillbilly who had the verbal skills of a banana slug. She had imagined at first they'd have an active social life—parties, going out. But all he wanted now was TV sports and beer and an occasional roll in the sack.

Gillian didn't mind having to do all the talking at the bar—it was what she was best at anyway. "I could really stand to slip out of here for a bowl of clam chowder." Give him a challenge, see what this man of action can handle.

"Got a suggestion?" he asked.

"Brigantine's got the best in town," she said, sliding off the barstool. *"It's quieter there anyway. We can talk—if you're not afraid of me."*

"I can always call a cop," he said, clearly intrigued but still cautious, still limp.

They got an early start in the morning, headed into the sun along Interstate 8 toward the Laguna Mountains.

"You're going to adore Julian," she said, leaning close, speaking over the wind noise filling the cockpit of Allen Neil's blue Miata roadster. *"It's a little ol' gold mining town out in the middle of nowhere."*

But their exploration of the tiny town doing its damnedest to be quaint was cursory. They quickly stopped pretending to be interested in anything other than the main reason they had come and checked in to the old hotel.

Gillian came from his left side, her knees pressing craters in the mattress. He raised his hand to the curve of her back, letting it slide over her ass. She leaned forward, her breasts brushing against his chest and his cock as she moved across him.

In the excitement of Allen's first time with her he would be throbbing in his groin. He'd be fighting, she knew, to retain control. He'd feel a pressure to explode he hadn't had since his teenage years. She knew the feel and smell of her would intoxicate him, as would the blaze of red hair framing her face and defining the V where her legs met. She moaned, partly from her own enjoyment of the prelude, but mostly with the pleasure of her control over him.

Neal marked his place and put the book aside in order to make a few notes. But before he could concentrate on writing, he drew a few deep breaths. He hated the thought of being turned on by this book, but he felt himself being aroused. He went to the sink and drew a glass of water and downed a pair of aspirin. Reading over his notes later, he realized that they didn't help his case one bit. *She's got my car identified,* Neal thought. *Brigantine for chowder; even her rationale for coming on like a nymphomaniac. So many details—like watching a videotape. Even the scar.*

Neal dialed home. "Sweetheart, I miss you already. Nothing to look forward to on this assignment. At least on a ship I could stop in the Orient—pick up some Noritake."

"What about the lawyer? Any good?" Yvonne asked, voice resigned.

"She says she is. Are the reporters leaving you alone?" he said.

"Mostly. They really hate being ignored, though. Have they found you yet?"

"I expect they'll be at the investigation." Neal realized that they were just swapping useless information, that at least for the moment their passion had been put on hold. That ought to be easy. They'd been on hold for years before. But it was harder now that he'd finally learned to love being together with Yvonne.

"They're doing promos on TV that the bitch is going to be on *Dagmar* Monday. That ought to sell her stinking book—supposing that those morons who watch that garbage can even read. God, Neal, this is like navy-sponsored extortion," Yvonne said, a mixture of anguish and anger in her tone. "How much of this are we supposed to take?"

How could he answer? There *were* no limits on what they could expect if the navy got embarrassed enough. Look at the lengths they had gone to in the USS *Iowa* gun turret explosion, blaming a lone sailor—even fabricating a gay lovers' quarrel to cover the errors and omissions of his superiors. "I just don't know."

NOW THAT HE WAS an official "geographical bachelor" with home and family elsewhere, Neal rated a two-room suite in the visiting officers' quarters. Comfortable enough. And unless someone talked, the media had little chance of finding him, even though the hotel-like structure was outside the base.

He leaned his head back on the couch and closed his eyes. He needed a break from the reading and note making. *Navy Wench* was embarrassing to read, but not just because of the sex. Too much of its portraits of navy wives and their husbands—and lovers—rang true. Regarding the book with a purely analytical eye as Lethajoy had instructed, Neal had to concede that Angela Vance had nailed the modern navy. Even though her bias came through on every page, he couldn't argue with most of what she said. No wonder the navy needed a patsy. Somehow, she had touched on virtually every major navy sex scandal in recent years. Sex in the Naval Academy dormitories; sex crimes committed against children; admirals accused of sexual harassment; and, of course, the Tailhook convention in Las Vegas, where unwilling women were forced to run a gauntlet of drunken male aviators.

He remembered Lethajoy saying, "There was the admiral who had been called out of retirement for a sexual harassment court-martial and was awarded thirty days' detention in officers' quarters. That renewed accusations of a double standard for officers and enlisted." Then she had added, "The admiral's kid glove punishment brought a howl from women's advocates since he had used his powerful position to victimize female subordinates. Who knows how many there were who had been too afraid to report him?"

ONCE THROUGH THE SAN Diego Naval Base main gate, Neal drove up Senn Avenue almost to Chollas Creek, to the naval legal center. The buildings at this end of the base, most relics of World War II or earlier, had the flat, drab utilitarian look of an industrial district. Sailors wearing the new working uniform that replaced dungarees—a deep blue shirt and trousers that would hold a crease—walked in the narrow streets, saluting as Neal passed. He felt vaguely fraudulent returning the courtesy, even though he wore the officer's uniform and rated the salute.

Across the bay, USS *Constellation* was in port snug against the carrier pier at North Island, larger than any other man-made thing on the horizon. Neal stopped the car and gazed over the water at the ship that had been his. Three years Neal had spent aboard the aircraft carrier. *Constellation—Connie—* he knew her by heart. He could literally find his way with his eyes closed through the labyrinth of decks and passageways. The ship, familiar as it had been, was now a stranger. *Just like I'm a stranger,* Neal said to himself. If he went aboard, few people would recognize him, the entire crew having turned over twice since his departure four years earlier from the flat top. And he felt even less connected now that the navy had tagged him for prosecution and humiliation.

Neal parked and walked to the quay wall fronting the Chollas Creek inlet, watching the early-morning preparations aboard the harbor tugs tied there. Diesel exhaust hung in the air while the marine engines deep in the tugs' hulls were tested and revved. Bo'suns coiled lines, laying them neatly on deck, while junior sailors rubbed polish on the brass fittings of the pilot house. Each knew what was expected; each could derive comfort from the certainty of his work. Neal turned away from the tugs and walked to the legal center's doors.

"COMMANDER, OF COURSE THERE'LL be no need for pretrial confinement or restriction. Just make yourself available during normal working hours." Captain Jules Watembach, commanding officer of the Naval Legal Service Office, wore a broad smile as he spoke from across his desk. He projected the demeanor of a doctor promising that all you're going to feel is a little pressure as he slips the needle between two vertebrae and sucks out the fluid that floats your brain. But the smile and tone did not camouflage his real meaning: If Neal disappeared, a federal bench warrant would be issued for him in a heartbeat. FBI, local cops. His treatment would become noticeably rougher.

"We ought to wrap this up pretty quickly and get you on the way to the rest of your life. I've detailed Lieutenant Junior Grade Barney Pilcher as your counsel. You'll like him. Sharp young man. Gonzaga graduate. Law review. Lots of enthusiasm."

"I also have civilian counsel, sir. Ms. Beltower. I take it that you know her," Neal said, sitting straighter in the chair in the captain's office, feeling like a new ensign.

"*Everybody* knows Beltower, Commander. She's something of an institution around here." Watembach stood, abruptly ending the meeting. "Pretrial investigation is set for this Wednesday. The investigating officer will be Captain August Thatcher, prospective commanding officer of one of the new underway replenishment ships going through outfitting down at National Steel. He had some time away from precommissioning duties, the shipyard had delays. He volunteered to help us out. Any reason you and Ms. Beltower can't make Wednesday, Commander?"

"Wednesday's fine, sir," Neal responded, trying to keep his tone friendly.

"Wonderful, Commander, wonderful. It gives you time for a haircut. We don't want to project a shaggy image in uniform, do we? Captain Thatcher is totally bald—a stickler." A small laugh. Watembach extended a hand across the desk, adding meat to his grin.

Guys like Watembach made Neal nervous. Laughing just before pushing you into the shark tank. *The sea service fraternity,* Neal thought, *the brotherhood of arms, if you happened to be the right brother and knew how to get along under the constant pressure of never knowing what a superior officer had in mind.* Would you be praised for initiative or put down for not knowing your place? Every action was a crap shoot. Junior officers, ensigns, jay gees were routinely admonished to reserve judgment until they knew the "big picture," an image that had never focused for Neal. By the time he had become a lieutenant commander, ten years into his career, he concluded that the elusive big picture was little more than window dressing hiding the fact that no one knew what the hell was going on.

"I EXPECTED THEY'D BRING in someone from the outside as investigating officer. I know most of the senior JAG types in the area," Lethajoy Beltower said, "with their dirty little secrets—" She stopped, grimaced and shook her head. "You don't need to hear this shit."

Monday, and Lethajoy was wearing dark green pants and a tight sweater that accentuated the jut of her breasts. Neal was mildly amused with himself, having halfway expected her to dress butch.

"It's the hypocrisy of it that twists my skivvies, 'til it gets too blatant and they have to act. Presidential elections don't help matters. All of them saying what they're going to do when they're president—things like gays in or gays out, litmus tests for the Joint Chiefs. Everybody talking about morality. . . ."

Neal unbuttoned his uniform jacket and loosened the black tie. He had never been particularly concerned about his weight. But the uniform he hadn't worn in a year now constricted. He wondered if his attorney had the habit of launching into these rants. Neal liked this woman but was not yet sure of her.

"It must have raised a red flag with the locals when I asked for your charge sheet. They went to battle stations. That part's OK—it gives us a psychological advantage. That applies to the appointed-defense end of this thing too. I don't know Barney Pilcher. It figures they'd assign junior counsel—lieutenant jay gee—won't have adult teeth yet." Lethajoy came around her desk and sat on the front corner. She had earlier noticed Neal admiring the desk and had said that her father, a retired chief petty officer, had collected hatch covers from wrecked sailing ships and had constructed it. He gave it to her when she passed the California bar.

"You think the prosecution will try getting Angela Vance to show up if she's off her book tour?" Neal asked. "From what she said, she still lives in this area—"

"Coronado. I looked her up. Still lives at the scene of the crime. The newspaper she used to write for had a piece bragging about their local girl. She must be giving the town populace heart failure." A laugh. "Every other house over there belongs to a retired admiral. She'd done features for the paper before getting famous so she'd had an opportunity to meet a lot of them, get close to the military community. Who knows, maybe she'll out one of *them* if *Navy Wench* sales drop off.

"The prosecution has the same problem we do. If she hasn't come right out and claimed what she wrote is true, it could trip them up. She tells the truth and she's screwed your pooch again. Any idea how much longer she'll be on the book tour?"

"Her publisher said mid-December," said Neal.

"Good. Let her stay mysterious and ghostly." The attorney regarded Neal with a thoughtful look for a few moments. "Does she have it in for you, any reason to think she wants to see you go down?"

"She never said anything. I think for her I was just an easy mark, someone to pay for her weekend amusement—"

"I'm serious about this. Was there anything that weekend that might have left her with a yen for revenge? Were you rough with her in any way?"

"What's the implication?" he asked, stiffening.

"Don't get all prickly on me. I've got to know what we're facing, and *I* wasn't in bed with her, *you* were. Now think about what you might have done—anything. It doesn't have to be about the sex. Did you disagree on politics, abortion, religion . . . women in the navy? Help me."

"I don't remember talking that much. . . . I was nervous. Just got promoted to commander. I'd been feeling pretty bad about Yvonne saying that she'd be filing for divorce. We hadn't had sex in months. . . . That's what I remember. A hard-on and an opportunity, to put it bluntly."

Lethajoy walked back to her side of the desk and sat down in her swivel chair. "Let's take a look at Angela Vance. Maybe that will stir some useful memories." She pointed to a portable television-VCR on a table by the wall, then clicked the remote on her desk.

"THERE'S BEEN TALK THAT your book is not a novel, that it's mostly true." Dagmar Renauld puts on her trademark puzzled look.

"That's what they say. All I can tell you is that I hear some people are squirming," Angela says, laughing. A hundred women laugh along. Camera scans faces. The few older men in the audience look grim.

"The navy is investigating a Commander Neal Olen. My sources tell me the charge is adultery—with *you*, Angela— because of what you've been saying about *Navy Wench*." Dagmar holds the book for a close-up of the dust jacket—a fouled anchor embedded in a pink heart over a navy-blue background. "Any truth to the charge?" Dagmar gives that big wink. "Any *hot* stuff going on there?"

Smiles all around, giggles from the audience. Angela leans forward, returning the wink. "I can't help what people think. I'm just a lonely scribe in my windowless garret, living on peanut butter and passion for my craft, you know." Angela puts a finger to her cheek.

"Almost everything else in *Navy Wench* can be verified— all the navy sex scandals." Dagmar leans closer to her guest. "Why so cagey on this one, Angela?"

"It's a *novel*, Dagmar, but it has to ring true, so I create the milieu using real elements."

"Are you saying that the real Commander Neal Olen is Commander Allen Neil in the book?"

"Anything's possible."

"DO WE HAVE TO watch this crap?" Neal stood, turned away from the television.

"Get used to it," Lethajoy murmured, pressing the remote to pause the show. "She can't get away with that evasiveness in court. If we get that far, I'll barbecue her ass, Neal. That's a promise. It's effective foreplay on television when you're trying to sucker people into buying your book. *Can't* help *what people think*," Lethajoy mimicked the author's innocent pronouncements. "Leave if you want, but I've got to watch it—it's what you pay me for, Neal." She leaned back in the swiveler.

Neal stared out the window. The industrial area around Lethajoy's office on 15th Street had fallen heir to the homeless displaced by the city's spruce-up. Below, at the mouth of an alley, Neal could see a bent figure in dirt-darkened clothing leaning into a dumpster. A small pile of his finds lay on the concrete by his feet.

He drew a breath and returned for the final few minutes of *Dagmar*. The deep breath, the pause, were part of the routine he'd been practicing more these days. He found himself regularly taking the time to impose calm on himself, to imagine his heart connected to a lever that he could use to slow its racing, consciously turning down his anger and fear. It was something he'd learned from a dentist aboard *Connie* during a cruise. The lever technique seemed to work better for Neal, though, when he had a mouthful of lidocaine and clouds of nitrous oxide up his nose.

Lethajoy leaned forward, snapping off the VCR. "Ready to bare your soul?"

Neal drew air through his nose and straightened in the chair. Full disclosure. Anathema, but he was past the point of being able to choose. "Where do you want me to start?"

CHAPTER SEVEN

When they arrived on base at 9 o'clock to meet with the navy-appointed defense counsel, there were no media people in evidence. "It's a little early for the buzzards," Lethajoy remarked. She was dressed in a powder blue business suit, wearing a hint of pink lipstick. "They usually come out only after the blood has been spilled. You've gotta be someone like Ken Starr to have 'em follow you. The worst thing you can do is not respect their news cycle. You ever plan to murder someone, do it early in the day."

"On the whole, I'd prefer skipping the entire mess. You suppose you can arrange that?" Neal remarked nervously as they approached the legal center.

"Come on, Commander, time to meet your defense team—see if he's had his pablum yet."

They stopped at the legal center reception desk and were directed to a room empty of everything but a table and four straight-backed chairs. Lethajoy, seated at the table, reviewed the file she had built so far on the case while Neal stood gazing out a window that had been dulled by diesel exhaust from the nearby tugs. Rivulets of rain had cleared a scattering of vertical tracks down the glass. The waterfront view refracted and wavered through the imperfect surface.

"Isn't he supposed to be here?" Neal asked, knowing damn well that his navy-appointed counsel was late, but not expecting an answer. He checked his watch: 0925. The appointment had been for 9 o'clock. At that moment the door swung partly open and a khaki-clad leg came through, then stopped. A hand gripped the doorsill. Neal could hear a snatch of soft, but unintelligible, conversation between the disembodied leg and hand and someone in the passageway.

The rest of the body pushed through the door, a six-foot-plus officer in his early twenties. Sandy crew cut and brown eyes. Athletic physique. The face was pasted with a serious look. He strode across the room in two paces, setting his slim briefcase on the table, extending a hand toward Neal. "Hi, Neal, I'm Barney Pilcher. I'll be representing you."

Neal regarded the officer but kept his own hands at his side. He hadn't cared when Lethajoy had suggested they use first names. But this was entirely different; retired or not, accused or not, he was still a senior naval officer in uniform. He could feel the hairs rise on his neck, being addressed in such a familiar way by a junior—very junior—officer who knew better. "My first name is Commander . . . Lieutenant," Neal said coldly, catching a glimpse of a grin on Lethajoy's lips.

"Sorry, I thought since we'd be working together. . . . If that's the way you want it, Commander, sir." Pilcher turned to Lethajoy uncertainly, hand still out. She looked up at him and took it with a perfunctory shake.

"Ms. Beltower is my lead defense attorney," Neal said, losing some of the ice in his voice.

"Well, sure, but I can take over easily at this point since we haven't started yet. It'll save you a bunch of bucks too, Commander." Pilcher dropped into a chair and snapped the catches on his briefcase. Inside, a single yellow legal pad—blank—and *A Guide to Military Criminal Law*. The slim volume had a pink Post-it protruding from between the pages.

Neither Neal nor Lethajoy spoke. Barney went on, glancing rapidly from one to the other. "Well, certainly we can be co-counsel, right?" He focused on Lethajoy. "I've already got the precedent," he said, sitting a bit straighter. "*U.S. versus Perez*. It was just like this case. Perez was separated from his wife and had sex with a civilian woman off base. Since there was no working relationship between them, Perez got acquitted on appeal. See, Commander, you've got nothing to worry about."

Lethajoy pushed her notes aside, leaning forward, forearms on the table. "You forgot that *Perez* was decided by the army appeals court on the question of prejudicial conduct. Navy's got its own appeals court that doesn't seem to care much for army precedent."

Barney was undeterred. "I'd argue the principle anyway. That, and that the adultery article is archaic."

"Is that how they do it at Gonzaga mock trials? And who was the jury there, a bunch of law students?" Lethajoy said, turning away.

In the small room they'd been assigned as defense headquarters, Neal watched the attorneys uneasily. "I'd appreciate some cooperation between you two."

When they were alone later Neal said, "I'm not sure I trust him—hell, I don't even like him. He's too eager. Had it all wrapped up before he even asked me a question. And what about this *Perez* case?"

Lethajoy confided to Neal, "I already looked at *Perez*. Might be some minor applicability but it's too early to settle on a defense theory. Got to see what they've got first. Barney is way ahead of where he ought to be. Once we get him tamed and he loses his delusions of controlling things, he could be an inroad to information. There are lots of loose lips around here. The guy probably doesn't even know what he knows that can be of real help . . . maybe he'll let slip with something."

CAPTAIN THATCHER, THE ARTICLE 32 investigating officer, carried himself with a confident set to his shoulders that belied his modest physical stature, making him seem taller and overcoming what could have been comical baldness above a pair of prodigious foxtail brows. As he entered the hearing room, Thatcher radiated the control of a Shakespearean actor taking possession of the stage.

The hearing room, however, bore none of the dignity of a courtroom. The nondescript space had the feel and smell of a small classroom, including a chalkboard on a side wall, a single window looking out on a parking area and a sliver of Coronado across the bay, a few tables, plastic and metal stacking chairs. It was unheated and chilly in the damp weather.

Aside from the court reporter, an enlisted woman, Captain Thatcher sat alone at one end of the room behind a table. That he was not accompanied by a navy lawyer indicated that he had a working knowledge of the pretrial investigation process and didn't need the assistance of a JAG officer at his elbow. As Lethajoy had merrily suggested, she had scared the little pricks away.

Captain Thatcher glanced around the hearing room, then cleared his throat. It was enough to bring instant attention. He paused, allowing the period of silence to establish the standard of conduct that he expected. The captain began speaking in a powerful voice. "We are here to determine the truth of charges preferred in the case of Commander Neal Edward Olen. This is an investigation into the truth of the charges, *not* a trial to assess guilt. My purpose is to act as an objective investigator and to make a recommendation as to the disposition of this case." Thatcher's voice rode on an undercurrent of crisp authority.

Neal sat in the center position at one of the two tables facing Thatcher. Lethajoy Beltower sat to Neal's left. Lieutenant Junior Grade Barney Pilcher sat to Neal's right, idly crosshatching his legal pad and filling in alternate squares with a felt-tip pen. The remaining table in the hearing room was occupied by a JAG Corps lieutenant commander who stood and identified himself to the room as Merlin Sutton, navy trial counsel. He would be the prosecutor, equivalent to a civilian district attorney. Sutton was rangy and loose-limbed. He was gray at the temples, probably in his mid-forties.

"Lieutenant Commander Sutton, proceed with your first witness," said Thatcher.

"Prosecution calls Special Agent Michael Godat, Naval Criminal Investigative Service, San Diego Field Office." Sutton took a step, pulled the hallway door open slightly. The door bumped wider a few seconds later as the NCIS special agent, packed into an extra-large blue blazer and gray slacks, walked in and crossed to stand in front of the witness chair near the end of Thatcher's table. Despite the chill in the room, a dark patch of perspiration showed under his raised arm as he was sworn in.

Agent Godat sat heavily, crossed his legs, exposing a calf like a sumo wrestler's. His unbuttoned blazer drooped to the side, revealing a small black holster attached to his trouser belt at the hip. Neal could see the butt of a revolver peeking out.

"What did you determine as a result of your inquiry?" Sutton asked.

Godat launched immediately into his role. "I concluded from documentary and broadcast evidence that it was likely the charges against Olen were accurate." His testimony was perfunctory.

"Ms. Beltower," Thatcher said when Sutton sat.

Lethajoy came to her feet, almost bouncing, and stepped toward the witness chair. "Agent Godat, this *documentary* evidence you say you found, did that include the book *Navy Wench*, written by Angela Vance?"

"Yes." Godat shifted in the chair, sighing, revealing, Neal imagined, an attitude about two of the least pleasant sides of his work: lawyers and women. Women lawyers. *Queer* women lawyers.

"Are you aware the book you identify as documentary evidence is a work of fiction?" Lethajoy said, ignoring the agent's blatant hostility.

"That doesn't make it untrue."

"Please answer yes or no, Agent," she said without humor, stepping closer.

"Yes, I *know* a novel is fiction." The tone of a teenager exasperated with the stupidity of a parent. Godat leaned back in the chair as if trying to put distance between himself and his questioner.

"In your investigation did you ever speak to Angela Vance?"

Godat methodically tugged his jacket sleeves over his thick wrists, taking his time. Forced nonchalance. "She wasn't available—she was traveling—so no."

Watching, Neal began to feel the discomfort the Criminal Investigative Service man was displaying. It was the same way Neal had felt whenever he was called to fill in as a last-minute replacement briefing officer for the admiral's morning intelligence assessment: not quite up to the second in his knowledge.

"Instead of actually talking to her you watched other people—TV interviewers—ask her questions." Lethajoy paused for a response that didn't come. "Couldn't you wait for her to come home? She lives just across the bay, you know. What was the rush?"

"I had limited time to complete my work," Godat responded.

"I see—you were *forced* to give your investigation short shrift." Now she was playing Godat specifically for Thatcher's benefit. "Let me be sure I understand. For your documentary evidence you relied on a work of fiction you believe to be true without ever having spoken to its author. Sounds like you were under intense pressure to complete your work regardless of its credibility."

"We're undermanned, so there's always pressure to finish. I stand behind any investigation that bears my signature." Godat sat a bit straighter.

"Yet you admit rushing through this one. Commander Olen was retired—it was not like there was any question of his availability. He wasn't about to leave on a ship or go overseas somewhere. So why was it so important to bring charges quickly?"

Exasperated, the agent sighed. "Just doing what I'm told."

"A classic response," she said, "one that has never worked in the past."

Sutton spoke up. "Objection. Characterizing the witness."

Lethajoy went on, not waiting for a ruling. "Agent Godat, have you ever spoken to Commander Olen?"

"He was out of the area."

"He lives about ten miles from the Port Hueneme Seabee Base NCIS office. Seems like you could have gotten an agent there to ask Commander Olen a few questions. Failing that, there is always the telephone. Is this how NCIS investigates?" Neal realized Lethajoy was trying to impeach not only the witness but the whole investigative service as well. And with good reason. Neal knew NCIS had a lousy reputation.

"We use a number of techniques." Godat shifted his mass in the chair.

"Do those techniques include television talk shows? You must watch a lot of television, Agent Godat. Must save a fortune on shoe leather."

"Objection," Sutton called out.

"Please stick to the questions, Ms. Beltower," Thatcher said.

"Yes, sir," she said, turning back to Godat. "I cannot understand your motivation here. *Why* did you conduct this investigation? It's not like you witnessed something."

"I was detailed by the special agent in charge of my office."

"Where did *his* direction come from?" Lethajoy said, feigning exasperation.

"Never asked."

"Now this is troubling, Agent. Your lack of curiosity as an investigator must be a handicap. There must have been some interest in serving justice from *somewhere* in the navy establishment for you to spend your time—limited and pressured though it was—on this search for truth. What do you suppose it might have been?"

"Objection—calls for speculation. Baiting the witness."

"No further questions of this witness, Captain," Lethajoy said quickly, dropping into her chair. Neal sensed her tension, her shortness of breath, like she had just run.

Agent Godat stood to leave. Captain Thatcher spoke. "Agent Godat, please sit down. I have some questions of my own." The NCIS agent hesitated, looked at Lieutenant Commander Sutton, then sat, still another sigh escaping like an inner tube losing air.

Thatcher nailed Godat with a stare. "In your investigation, did you find any direct evidence to support the adultery charge, say, credit card records for a hotel, witnesses who can put Commander Olen and Ms. Vance together? Any documentary or testimonial evidence like that?"

"No, sir."

Godat's answer clearly displeased the captain. "Agent, would you, if you had the authority, press charges based on the shaky evidence you brought here today?"

"My job is to—"

"Agent, I know what your job is, perhaps as well as you do," Thatcher said quickly, anger creeping into his tone. "Now since this is an informal setting, let's try again. Would you press charges if you had the authority?"

Godat looked toward Sutton, who suddenly had something of interest to attend to in his briefcase. Thatcher persisted. "I know you aren't a lawyer, Agent Godat, but it should be a simple question for a professional investigator."

Godat twisted in the chair and dragged a hand across his chin. "Without Angela Vance's statement—which I expect we'll get at court-martial when she can be subpoenaed—the evidence is not yet convincing. But there is the possible revelation of government secrets by the accused that is still under investigation."

Lethajoy shot to her feet, followed by Sutton. "Objection," she boomed, voice strident, taking a step as if to round the table for attack. "I strenuously object. There's been no prior mention of this *investigation*, no charge. It's irrelevant and prejudicial. And," she turned her head toward Sutton, face radiating anger, "it has all the earmarks of prosecutorial skullduggery."

Neal stiffened. He had hesitated to even think of it, had put it out of his mind following the *Story Line* interview, when Angela had hinted at having "sources." He hadn't mentioned it to Lethajoy since there had been no charges filed.

Under investigation for passing government secrets. The words left Neal gasping, like a fist to the gut. Having gone over and over in his mind his time with Angela, he was almost positive he hadn't compromised any classified information. Not only was it treasonous, it was a point of honor with him.

"Captain Thatcher," Sutton said, himself appearing bewildered, "I knew nothing of this before this moment."

"Agent, I would have presumed you'd know better," Thatcher said, addressing the NCIS man.

Godat cast his gaze at the floor, then after a moment raised his head, staring directly at the captain. "There wasn't enough yet for a charge. The book, *Navy Wench*, is under review by Naval Intelligence in Washington. They find evidence of an intelligence compromise and there'll be appropriate charges developed."

"If there is no evidence as of now, why would you even mention it here? What can your purpose possibly be, Agent?" Thatcher said.

"Slip of the tongue is all," Godat answered.

Thatcher paused, collecting his thoughts. "Counsel, you can both sit down. Agent Godat, I'll ignore your unfortunate comment and ask you again: would you have preferred charges of adultery based on the information you gathered? Yes or no. One word, please, Agent."

Godat looked at the floor, lips pursed, thumb moving over fingers of his left hand. "No," he said finally.

Captain Thatcher leaned back in his chair. Shaking his head he asked, "Does the government have further questions for this witness?"

"No, sir." Sutton spoke without enthusiasm. Now the exasperation was his. His case had been sidetracked, taken away from his control.

"Defense?"

"No, sir, but I do have a point of order," Lethajoy answered, rising, her voice once again moderated. "Captain Thatcher, one name seems to be missing from the witness list, sir." She held up a single sheet of paper. "Legalman Second Class Christopher Hamby. His name and signature are on the charge sheet as the accuser." She paused and stared pointedly at Sutton. "It is probably just an oversight." Neal watched Sutton's barely perceptible wince at the dig. "I took the liberty, Captain, of verifying that Petty Officer Hamby works in this very building and is now here and was available even before we began today." She turned toward Sutton. "Trial counsel can offer information on that, sir. Petty Officer Hamby is his subordinate."

"Commander Sutton," Thatcher said, "I'm interested why the accuser is not on the list, which is quite short in any case."

"Excuse me, Captain? Excuse me?" Godat was raising a hand, waving. "Are you done with me?"

"You're dismissed."

"Captain," Sutton began, running his finger down a page in the *Manual for Courts-Martial*, stopping. "Rule for Courts-Martial 405 only requires the accused be *informed* of the identity of the accuser."

Thatcher came back immediately. "Since availability and time are not an issue for a witness who's in the building, I think Ms. Beltower's request to question the accuser is perfectly reasonable. We'll recess for fifteen minutes, Commander Sutton."

"Check your office, Merlin. I'll bet he's somewhere in there," Lethajoy offered in a stage whisper. Sutton cast a cold stare. She turned to Neal and leaned close to his ear. Barney Pilcher strained his neck trying to hear. "Merlin is their sacrificial lamb. Nobody in the JAG Corps will shed a tear if he bombs. They need a kamikaze on this one. The Hamby thing is just a technicality, not a fatal error, but it points to a sloppy case. Probably won't kill the charges but who knows," Lethajoy said to Neal with a chuckle. Pilcher rose and wandered past Neal, mumbling about getting a Coke.

Neal couldn't see Barney's expression. It could be easily imagined, though he could not care a whit if Pilcher felt squeezed out. He had been thinking about the witness list and a particular name on it, and where he knew it from. *Kenneth Hoopingartner*—listed as the husband of Angela Vance. He pulled the witness list toward him. Following Godat's name, there it was, and he knew now for sure, four years later. He touched Lethajoy's arm, and she twisted in the chair to face him. "I know Hoopingartner. He was aboard *Constellation*. I had no idea they were married then. Hoopingartner worked in the intelligence film processing lab. He's a first class photographer's mate. I just made the connection. This could be trouble."

"Tell me quick. Whisper." She leaned in close.

"It's in the book—Gillian says her husband's away for a three-month school in Pensacola. That's the photography school. Hoopingartner was at an advanced course in equipment maintenance, video production . . . I don't remember exactly."

"Did she ever use the name Hoopingartner?"

"No, just Vance," Neal whispered.

The attorney thought for a moment. "OK, we'll deal with that." She turned her chair to face him closely. "What I'm more concerned about is the classified information Godat brought up. What is that and why did I have to find out here, now?" she asked.

Neal sighed. "In *Navy Wench*, chapter six—'my chapter'— there's some pillow talk about reconnaissance satellites. Used to be top-secret code word stuff about the Keyhole satellite system. But it's all been declassified now except for the overhead time schedule. Even so, I wouldn't talk about it."

"Is there any other potentially classified information in the book?" Lethajoy asked.

"Nothing that I recognized," Neal said.

"Looks like Godat alerted on the mention of recon satellites and kicked it up to Washington for the experts to look at it," Lethajoy said, continuing to whisper. "Still, it doesn't look good, you being in navy intelligence at the time and her writing pseudosecret stuff."

"So what do we do about it?" Neal asked.

"Nothing at the moment. Until it's an actual charge, it might as well be a rumor," she answered. As Sutton neared their table, returning from his mission to fetch Petty Officer Hamby, Lethajoy raised her voice to normal. "Some damn associate counsel we've got. Went out for a Coke and didn't even offer to get us one."

SUTTON WORE A GRIM face as he swore in Petty Officer Hamby.

"Are you the accuser in this case?"

"Yes, sir," the young sailor answered, wearing a puzzled look.

"How did you come to be knowledgeable enough to sign the preferral of charges?"

"There was an NCIS investigation, sir."

"No further questions."

Thatcher eyed Sutton. "There *must* be more questions, Commander—this *is* the accuser on the witness stand."

"No more questions, sir." Was Sutton pouting, or could it be just Neal's imagination?

"Ms. Beltower, I expect you'll have a query or two." There was the shadow of a smile on Thatcher's face.

"Indeed, sir." She rose. "Petty Officer Hamby, aside from the Naval Criminal Investigative Service report that you cited, do you have any other personal knowledge of this case?"

"No, ma'am. I just typed the charge sheet."

"Yet your signature and oath appear on the charge sheet, and you just repeated that oath for us today."

"I was told to sign the sheet."

Sutton rose. "Sir, if I might, I think I can clear this up."

"Go ahead, Commander, but I'm disappointed you did not feel compelled to 'clear it up' during your direct examination when the opportunity was ripe," Thatcher said.

Sutton spread his arms, gesturing that he was going to give a simple answer, one that the others should have divined without his help. "Since Agent Godat is a civilian and not subject to military law, it is common practice to have a surrogate stand in as accuser. It's just a paperwork convenience."

Thatcher nodded toward Lethajoy. "Ms. Beltower?"

"Thank you, Captain. For the accuser to have no under-standing of the charges to which he has signed his name and sworn—to not even have read the investigation—is taking expediency a bit far." Lethajoy turned toward Thatcher. "Sir, I move for a recommendation of dismissal of all charges under Rule 307, paragraph b, Preferral of Charges."

Sutton glared but kept silent.

Neal understood now that there was more than just the fear Lethajoy would expose JAG Corps sexual peccadil-loes—she was a damn good attorney. She must have mem-orized the *Manual for Courts-Martial.*

Seconds passed. Lethajoy stood squarely facing Thatcher.

The captain spoke. "I'll take that motion under advise-ment when I prepare my report. Thank you, counselor. Do you have any further questions for the witness?"

"No, sir. That would require a presupposition that Legal-man Hamby actually *knows* something." Lethajoy returned to her seat. As she took the chair, Neal could feel an aura around her, an excitement that he hadn't detected before. The glow of a small victory? Like a soccer goal.

"Commander Sutton, if you are through with Petty Offi-cer Hamby, please call your final witness."

Photographer's Mate First Class Kenneth Hoopingart-ner, the size and shape of a well-toned halfback, strode in, took the witness chair, gripping the arms, and stared at Neal with tight mouth and furrowed brow.

Neal kept a neutral face, focusing on the six neat rows of three ribbons each on the big sailor's chest, evidence that the services increasingly used the awards as consolation prizes for long hours, low pay and family separations. He remembered wardroom conversations—officers decrying the proliferation of routine decorations that merely cheapened those that were earned through effort.

"Where are you currently stationed, Petty Officer Hoopingartner?" Sutton asked.

"Fleet Imaging Center, North Island."

"And before that?"

"USS *Constellation*, Photography Division, reconnaissance film processing lab in the Carrier Intelligence Center."

"What period were you married to Angela Vance?"

"July 1993 until October '97," Hoopingartner responded, propping his elbows on the chair arms, looking ready to push off for a dash to the door or perhaps a charge across the twenty-five feet that separated him from Neal.

"What was your relationship to Commander Olen?" Sutton asked.

"He was the *Connie's* intelligence officer. He ran the Intelligence Division. His office was in the Intelligence Center where I worked."

"In fact, didn't you have to pass the door of Commander Olen's office to get to the film lab?"

"Yes, sir," Hoopingartner answered, voice flat.

"Have you read *Navy Wench*?"

"It's all bullshit. Pissed me off." Hoopingartner thrust forward, face reddening.

Sutton let the language pass. "This is very important, Petty Officer Hoopingartner, since the book was written about the period when Angela Vance was your wife. What is your assessment of the truth of the story in *Navy Wench*, even though it is purportedly wrapped in the cloak of fiction?"

"Seems true to me, sir, like all she did was put new names on people." The petty officer thought for a moment.

"Gillian Lorenz, the woman in the book, is just like Angela—like a clone." He paused and looked at the floor, then raised his eyes to Neal, snapping with anger. "Couple of sluts."

"Objection." Lethajoy was on her feet. "Both the question and the answer lack relevance. 'How true is fiction?' 'Seems true.' This is nothing more than a game of let's make something up and go to court. . . ."

"Ms. Beltower, please. I understand your objection," Thatcher said, irritation edging his words. "You needn't go on. Commander Sutton, can we get past this book and have some testimony of substance?"

Sutton picked up questioning. "Petty Officer Hoopingartner, was Commander Olen your division officer, in your chain of command?"

"No, sir. Commander Olen was in charge of Intelligence Division. I was in Photographic Division under Ensign Aschman."

"But you worked in Intelligence Division spaces and Ensign Aschman's office was in the ship's regular photo lab six decks below," Sutton said.

"Yeah, I didn't normally see Ensign Aschman except for muster in the morning. I was the senior man in the lab and he left me alone unless there was some problem."

"Where did you get your day-to-day orders from?"

"The assistant intelligence officer, Lieutenant Fulton," Hoopingartner answered matter-of-factly.

"And Lieutenant Fulton was directly under Commander Olen?"

"Yes, sir."

"So, even though—on paper—you were not in Commander Olen's chain of command," Sutton said slowly, making his point, "you worked in Intelligence Division spaces and responded to his work orders and those of his assistant division officer? Commander Olen was your de facto division officer?"

"I guess."

"No more questions."

"Ms. Beltower, your turn," Thatcher said.

Sutton was giving Thatcher a solid reason to forward the charges for court-martial, something beyond the earlier vague assertions of "true fiction," Neal thought. Testimonial evidence, finally, that would support both the charge of conduct unbecoming an officer and the adultery charge, what this thing was really all about—screwing a subordinate's wife. Moral turpitude, compromising an officer's standing before his subordinates.

Lethajoy rose slowly. "Petty Officer Hoopingartner, when did you become aware of the allegation that Commander Olen had sexual relations with your wife?"

"Two months ago. I saw her on television."

"And did this make you angry?" Lethajoy spoke like a shrink, softly, a friend just trying to help.

"Nobody wants the boss screwing his wife."

"But you haven't been married to Angela Vance for more than two years. Are you now married to someone else?"

"Yes, ma'am." Hoopingartner seemed to be calming.

"You testified just now that you have known of the alleged tryst for two months—about the time Angela Vance started showing up all over television. About the time it became clear that she was going to become a rich woman from her book sales. Did Angela ever personally tell you anything about her and Commander Olen?"

"No."

"Then I'm puzzled, Petty Officer Hoopingartner. I don't understand what you were angry about. This was something that allegedly happened four years ago, something that never had—even if it did happen—any effect on your work in the navy, in either Photography or Intelligence Division, or in your relationship with Commander Olen, or even your relationship with your wife at the time, Angela Vance?"

"I didn't like being played for a fool. . . ."

"Four years later? Isn't it possible your anger stems from missing out on Angela's newfound wealth? Those book royalties."

"Objection, argumentative," Sutton said from his table.

"I'll allow it," Thatcher said, leaning forward.

The petty officer's face hardened and he spat his answer at Lethajoy. "That's crap."

"We're nearly finished, Petty Officer, if you'll bear with me. I'm curious about the nature of your marriage—for instance, why Angela Vance did not go by even a combined name the way women do these days?"

The sailor clenched his fists on the chair arms. Lethajoy had probed an unexpectedly tender spot.

"She said it was too long, it sounded funny. She didn't want to give up her *identity*. Vance was a better name for a writer, looked better in print, she said." He recited the answer quickly, flatly.

"Sounds like a great way to start a marriage—"

"Fuck her and fuck you!"

"Petty Officer Hoopingartner," Thatcher snapped. "Any further language or attitude like that and you'll be put on report. Article 134 . . . ," the captain paused.

". . . paragraph 89, sir," Lethajoy finished the captain's sentence, supplying the correct charge, just one of the fifty-six ways to violate the General Article, or what some called the "Elastic Article"—from adultery to wearing unauthorized insignia, the article could always be stretched to fit a given situation.

"Sorry, *sir*," Hoopingartner squeezed the words past clenched teeth, pointedly avoiding Lethajoy in his apology.

She went on. "Let's talk about something else since this discussion about your name seems to be a painful subject for you, Petty Officer Hoopingartner. You testified earlier that the story in *Navy Wench* seemed true to you. Does that truth include the character portrayed as Gillian's husband, Ken—same as your first name, isn't it—Ken? The man Gillian married was a drinker, and an uncommunicative wife abuser. Is that a *true* description of you?"

"No." The man's face reddened.

"But it's in the book."

"I said no!" Hoopingartner was now leaning forward like a racer in starting blocks.

"Then how can you be assured that Allen Neil is a true description of Neal Olen—that the actions of Olen and Allen are the same, that in fact anything in the book is true?"

"I can't," Hoopingartner finally said.

"No more questions."

LETHAJOY ELBOWED HER WAY through the gathered reporters outside the legal center building, leading the way for Neal like a downfield blocker, Barney Pilcher falling in behind. To the babble of questions she smiled and answered, "When this is over, we'll have a statement. As of now, it is not over."

"Commander," someone called out from the knot of video cameras and microphones, "will there be a court-martial?"

"You have an affair with Angela Vance, Commander?" another cried, jostling for position.

In his growing dislike for newspeople, an emotion that had been spurred by the incident outside his home, Neal drew a blank expression and said nothing. They could make of it what they would.

CHAPTER EIGHT

That evening, Neal and Lethajoy met to discuss strategy over dinner at a San Diego waterfront restaurant, À la Bonne Heure. Bay waters lapped the sea wall across the promenade. Aromas of mesquite smoke and beef steaks filled the room. It seemed a little tony for a business meeting, but Lethajoy had insisted. As they were having drinks and salads, a slender woman approached their table. She was dressed in the black-and-white checked trousers and white smock of a chef. Her chestnut hair was tucked under a tall toque.

Lethajoy introduced the woman as Susan Lamply, her "companion." Neal stood and took Susan's hand. "A pleasure to meet you, Susan," he said, immediately taken with her fine features and serene demeanor. She was not like anyone he could imagine having just emerged from a busy restaurant kitchen.

"Lethajoy's told me about your case," Susan said. "I hope it all works out."

"Susan spends so much time here that coming by's the only way I can see her most nights," Lethajoy said. "Food's not bad, either."

Susan returned to her work, having assured Neal that she would personally prepare his Steak Diane.

Lethajoy said, "It looks like Thatcher isn't going to be swayed by Sutton's bullshit. I almost feel sorry for ol' Merlin, but I'd run a saber through his heart in a second." She took a bite of her field greens salad. "How are you holding up, Neal? Talked to your wife?"

"I'll call her when we're done here." Neal wondered how much Lethajoy needed to know, how much he should spill for his own mental health, if not for development of his defense. He quickly decided not to burden her with anything else that might distract from the proceedings. He'd never believed in all that crap about the value of talk, talk, talk, getting his emotions, his innermost feelings out. Besides, she was a lawyer, not a shrink.

"I was thinking, since Angela concealed the fact she was married, doesn't that have some bearing? Isn't that a mistake of fact? I couldn't have known she was Hoopingartner's wife."

"Nice try, Neal, but you would also have to forget that *you* were married. Are you willing to try convincing a judge of that?" She laid the fork across the salad plate. "If they put every sailor who cheated on his wife in jail, there wouldn't be a ship that could get under way. Look, that's the kind of thing that galls me. Take a guy away from his family for half a year, drop him in some liberty port like Subic Bay where the main industry is liquor and prostitution. He succumbs to temptation and breaks military law. Don't get me wrong. That's no excuse for screwing around on your wife—or husband—but it does come off just a bit hypocritical. I'm not making an excuse for you, Neal, but what you did is not worth prison time."

Neal listened to his attorney's indictment. Nothing he could say against the truth. "Hypothetically, what could really happen if I were to just own up to it?"

"You mean a plea bargain?" He nodded. Lethajoy regarded her client silently before speaking. "It's a decision only you can make, and it might come out a good one, but on balance I suggest that you wait to make any decision like that. Look, the possibility exists that Thatcher will make it all go away. But if you plead now, you forfeit in the first inning."

Neal had to consider the effect a guilty plea would have on Yvonne. He'd be redeeming his honor at her expense. "It's frustrating to just sit, listening to Sutton. I want to say something," he said.

"You'll have your chance to talk tomorrow, Neal."

"WELL?" YVONNE SAID, voice eager, apprehensive.

"Nothing yet. The lawyer thinks we may have a chance of avoiding court-martial, the way things are going with the investigating officer."

"Even with . . ."

"There's no proof." The telephone lines transmitted their silence for half a minute. "What say we head up toward Ojai, have dinner Saturday? Forget all this garbage for a while," Neal offered.

"I'd love that. I'm beginning to feel like a prisoner."

"Honey, I miss you. We can pretend Ojai is on Mars—" Neal realized that his fondest wish could come true with an airplane ticket out of the country. Losing this case would mean he and Yvonne would have no life left in California. No reason to stay. Running away had never been an option he'd seriously considered before. He'd been too well indoctrinated by the navy, where even being late for work was a crime.

In his Visiting Officers' Quarters room, lights dimmed, occasional muted footsteps in the passageway outside the door, Neal wrestled with what moral decisions he had faced back then in Coronado. Would he have gone with Angela that night had he known she was Mrs. Hoopingartner? Probably not. What was a reasonably responsible officer-like approach to the situation of dinner, drinks and a hard-on? Would a prudent officer have tried to find out if she was married and therefore—he laughed aloud at the word that the question brought to his mind, a word he hadn't used since college: *jailbait*. Thirty-something jailbait in a gauzy skirt.

NEAL STRODE TO THE witness chair and sat at attention. "Captain Thatcher, as you can imagine, this whole episode has been difficult for me. My marriage has been threatened, and I'm facing financial ruin. My security clearances were suspended, and I lost my job. I feel powerless to defend my-self, sir—I'm battling ghosts." Neal was talking too fast. He drew a breath, slowed.

"The case against me relies on a testimony of guesswork and belief rather than fact. I respectfully request that you rec-ommend against court-martial and that all charges be dropped." Pressure, a throbbing, low in his forehead, threat-ened tears. But even as emotion tinged Neal's words he ended with head up and eyes locked on the investigating officer.

"Is that all, Commander?" Thatcher asked quietly.

"Yes, sir. I have nothing else."

"Prosecution, do you have a closing argument?"

Sutton began. "Sir, we find ourselves in an odd position. Other than the accused, who chooses to exercise his right to make a statement and not to be questioned, only one other person can knowledgeably testify to what occurred in No-vember of 1995: Angela Vance.

"There is sufficient reason to believe that the charges are true. However, there are only two ways we will ever find out—if Commander Olen chooses to confess or a court-martial authority subpoenas Angela Vance and compels her testimony." Merlin Sutton had begun a slow stroll immediately in front of Thatcher's table. "Therefore, I respectfully call for you to refer this case to the convening authority with a recommendation to go forward with the court-martial of Commander Neal Edward Olen."

Sutton glanced at Lethajoy, turning up the corners of his mouth—a victory grin.

"Ms. Beltower?" Thatcher said, lifting his eyebrows.

"Thank you, Captain," Lethajoy answered, rising. She planted her hands on the table before her and leaned forward. "From the beginning, this case has reeked like a truckload of rotten fish. And now we are told that it's *impossible* for the prosecution to make a case with the witnesses it has produced." She glanced at the prosecutor. "I am astonished that any JAG Corps officer could speak those words and then smile as Commander Sutton just did." She stepped around the defense table. "Agent Godat admitted that his investigation was slapdash and he relied on television talk shows and *Navy Wench*, a book of fiction. Perhaps if his investigation had not been handled at warp speed, Agent Godat could have produced Ms. Vance or at least some of her *nonfiction* words in a statement." Lethajoy now turned, facing Sutton. "And for a prosecution witness to make vague allegations about secret material being compromised. . . ." She shook her head. "That's just irresponsible."

Thatcher broke in. "Be assured, Ms. Beltower, that I will take Agent Godat's testimony, all of it, into consideration. Continue."

"Even if the alleged adultery had happened, it sent no shock waves through the navy, because until two months ago, nobody had even imagined it. The *imagination* was in this novel," Lethajoy held up the book, "supplied by Angela Vance, a shameless self-promoter. That, Captain, is the truth of the matter."

Neal leaned forward, wanting to smile at his lawyer's argument, her way of building it without forsaking an opportunity to take a shot at Merlin Sutton. He drew his mouth down, cutting off any expression other than serious, concerned.

"Commander Sutton pleads that *only* Angela Vance can make his case and that will take a court-martial because of his lack of subpoena power over civilians. I wonder whether he bothered to simply ask her to voluntarily show up for this investigation, where her denial would end things once and for all. As Commander Sutton knows, a court-martial makes for a better show! And isn't a show what the prosecution wants—win or lose?" Lethajoy paused to sip from her water glass, allowing her theory to hang in the air.

"Captain Thatcher, I agree with Commander Sutton on one point that he made in his closing statement—that there is no case! I respectfully request that your recommendation to the convening authority be for full dismissal of all charges and carry an instruction to the Defense Security Service to restore Commander Olen's security clearance."

THE ROUNDUP RANCH RESTAURANT near Ojai was probably more expensive than they should have gone for, but Yvonne had suggested their return to the landmark eatery. The Roundup Ranch had been where Jarrel and Martha Schneider had taken them for a welcome-aboard dinner when they had arrived in Camarillo from Hawaii—when there had been excitement and optimism. When their post-navy life held a bright promise.

"I know that Jarrel dying wasn't my fault," Neal said, once they'd been seated at the restaurant, "but I feel bad about the whole situation anyway. He was a decent guy, once you got past the bluster."

"That must have been only at work. I never saw it. He was always so gallant with me."

Neal chuckled. "The old man had an eye for beautiful women. Glad he was harmless." He reached for Yvonne's hand.

They sat outside with a view of the Topa Topa Mountains. Pleasant warmth radiated from heaters on poles, like parasols with glowing, gas-fired centers. Carefully kept flower and herb gardens, naturalistic landscaping and a running brook invited diners to linger after they had eaten, to stroll the paths. The smell of roses filled the cool night air.

"I've been checking with the school district employment office. Nothing full-time available this early in the year—other than high school wood shop and a French class." Yvonne related her week in an animated tumble of words. "I'm going to interview for elementary grades substitute. Something will open soon, they said; someone's always leaving or out pregnant."

Neal gazed across the small table at his wife, a white knitted shawl draped gracefully across her shoulders. She appeared to be holding up under the pressure of uncertainty. But how would she handle his conviction and prison sentence if it came to that? The bugaboo that had haunted their marriage before, a long separation, could crawl into their lives again. She had chosen to address his absence on the ship the last time by filing for divorce. Is that how she'd respond again, no matter that she was supporting him now? Could he blame her if she did?

Yvonne sipped her coffee while Neal had a tiny glass of Sambucca, served as he remembered it in Italy, with three coffee beans representing good health or good luck.

Afterward, they wandered up a narrow path to the meditation bench at the top of the garden. The air kept its chill here at the stone bench, and they leaned close together, touching shoulders.

"You've been so quiet, more so than normal," she said.

"It's always been easy to talk in the past. Just talk about work—about nothing. Everything in life laid out neat, logical. I've got no control now. I've turned my life over to Lethajoy Beltower, Esquire, and I watch from the sidelines." Neal thought a moment about his attorney, her spirit and confidence. Her anger. "She seems to be doing a good job, made some damn good points, but who knows. She might be letting some of what she feels about the navy and the way they made her resign color her presentation."

Yvonne put a hand on his forearm. "You want a new lawyer? What about the navy lawyer, Pilcher?"

"Galoof," he said with a slight laugh. Yvonne looked at him quizzically. After a pause he went on. "I haven't thought of that word in years. What Mom called the jerks who gave her hassles in the casino. Galoofs. Wasn't 'til I was in college that I realized she meant 'galoot.'" He sighed, remembering his childhood embarrassment of seeing his mother in her brief cocktail runner costume.

"Anyway, Pilcher's just a young kid. Doesn't seem to care much one way or the other. Maybe it's because his job is to keep quiet when what he really wants is to taste blood. It would probably be his own blood, along with mine, if he presented the case." Neal wagged his head slowly, pursing his lips. "I see him hanging around with some JAG types that are definitely not friendly to my case. Maybe it's just my imagination but I don't trust him. Anyway, Lethajoy seems competent, definitely smart, and I'll bet Thatcher thought so, too, when she gave her closing argument." He leaned back and immediately felt the stone bench chill his skin through his jacket and shirt. "Guess we'll see Monday if Thatcher was impressed."

Yvonne leaned back, tipping her head to his shoulder. The fragrance of her hair drew him to bury his face in it. After a minute he laid his head back, filling his vision with a star-pierced sky. The clarity of the atmosphere at this elevation brought to mind the crystal nights of his youth in the Nevada high desert.

"Did I ever tell you about when my dad left us? Mom made Rich the man of the house. I was still the kid."

"I could never get you to say much about your childhood," Yvonne murmured, leaning into his shoulder.

Neal drew a slow breath. "Guess I was embarrassed. Now I can look at the old man and admit that he was a real jerk. Had me fooled back then, but what can you expect from an eleven-year-old? All I knew was that he made us laugh, sometimes." Neal picked up a twig and methodically removed the bark as he spoke. "Once he took us waterskiing. Borrowed a boat and proceeded to get drunk and stay that way all weekend. Never did get to ski." Neal rolled out the story of the waterskiing trip, the terror of riding in the boat as his drunken father spun wildly through tight turns, the outboard screaming as the propeller cavitated at full speed. "Anyway, that's when Rich had his great awakening. Realized that he could pretty much do what he wanted because he could intimidate Mom, and Dad really didn't care. By that time he was bigger than Dad even though he was only fourteen. And when Dad bailed out on us, Rich just got worse. Mom couldn't control him so she just ignored him."

Yvonne laid a hand across Neal's leg as he talked and stroked a small area with her thumb, as though she could rub away his painful memory.

"The asshole turned me into his slave. Eventually he went into the army." Neal laid his hand over Yvonne's and sighed. "He was invited to join up by a local judge. Army or jail. What a sweet revenge that was. Mom and I got a couple years of freedom, and Rich got thumped on a regular basis by his drill sergeant. Got a letter from him once. Seems that there was this U.S. Army conspiracy against him. Everybody in authority was a stupid jerk." Neal gave a short laugh. "Wish I'd saved that letter. Funny thing is, at the moment I might agree with him—sure feels like a conspiracy.

"Anyway, when I went off to college, Mom found a better cocktail job in a Stateline casino. She was a back bar assistant. Moved to an efficiency apartment up in South Lake Tahoe. She was starting to show her age, close to fifty, and only the drunkest players showed enough interest to try copping a feel and would as likely make insulting remarks."

Yvonne said, "I can't imagine what that must have done to her."

"Got so she wouldn't put up with shit from anyone. Just got tired of it, I guess. Even what few tips she'd get went way down." Neal leaned forward, staring at the ground beneath his shoes and the leaves that skittered along in the light breeze.

"I never told her about Rich, the way he constantly intimidated me, but she had to know—had to see the bruises. And when Dad left, after a while nobody talked about him anymore, like he had never been there. I didn't realize it until I was an adult that sure, Mom got increasingly bitter, but she never abandoned us."

A sob constricted his throat and he turned away. Yvonne put a hand on his shoulder and drew him close, her lips softly at his ear. The revelation to his wife and his sudden and full acceptance of it slammed through his mind—an admission finally of what he had ignored for thirty years.

A brilliant, self-destructive father who disappeared into the night forever.

A mother who could barely read, worked the Lucky Buck, and stayed with her children.

Take your pick, Neal said to himself later, as if there'd ever been a choice for any of them.

As they returned to Spanish Hills from Ojai, a kind of fatalism filled the car. Silence broken by Neal's grunting recognition in response to Yvonne's observations of banal details along the road—the construction work on the Victoria Avenue interchange, an SUV tailgating a vintage Volkswagen bus, someone changing a tire in the median. Like a first date on its way to being the last.

"What'll you do if I end up in prison?" He kept his eyes straight ahead, as if by doing so he could avoid further emotional contact. He immediately wished he hadn't asked. Still, he had to know, had to understand what the consequence to his marriage would be if a guilty verdict were handed down.

"How can you ask me that? How can I possibly know? Didn't you say that the article whatever investigation went OK? Are you changing your story now?" Hurt and anger colored Yvonne's words.

He knew better than to pursue this, to give in to his penchant to explore every possibility, every detail.

They crossed the Santa Clara River, the Miata's tires setting up a rhythm, slapping the expansion strips in the concrete in double beat.

"Is this more of your contingency planning?" Yvonne said.

"We hadn't discussed it before, Yvonne. I need to know what you'd do, worst case."

"I don't even want to think about it now. I've been thinking of everything but."

CHAPTER NINE

In the hearing room waiting for the investigating officer, Neal could muster slight confidence. Lethajoy had met him on the way in. She was wearing a dark blue skirt and jacket nearly the color of his uniform. She gave him a smile, but she said nothing as they took their seats. He guessed that nerves had captured her as well.

Neal had nothing he could do to pass the minutes except notice the trickle of sweat tracking from his armpit down his side. He scraped his thumbnail over a rough spot on his left hand, creating a flap of skin that, moved a fraction of an inch further, would produce blood.

"Attention on deck!" Sutton called as Captain Thatcher entered the hearing room.

"Carry on," Thatcher said immediately, automatically, before the room's occupants could half rise from their chairs. He took his seat.

Neal's stomach tightened. Lethajoy touched his sleeve.

"These proceedings are reconvened at 1305, Monday, December 20, 1999." Captain Thatcher placed his briefcase on the table and drew out a stack of papers—the NCIS investigation, Article 32 hearing transcripts, charge sheet—and laid his hand on them. Thatcher scanned the room, looking from Sutton to Lethajoy and finally to Neal. "After careful consideration of the evidence presented, I have concluded that the appropriate disposal of this case is dismissal. My recommendation to the convening authority is that all charges be dropped and Commander Olen's clearances be reinstated."

Neal's chest expanded as he took a deep breath. He could feel Lethajoy's hand gripping his forearm.

"But, sir." Sutton was standing, moving forward a pace.

Captain Thatcher nailed Sutton with a stare that stopped the prosecutor. "Commander Olen, owing to the Christmas season, I would expect the convening authority to make its endorsement early in January. Until you are officially released, you remain on active duty but may stay at your home on administrative leave until further notice. Thatcher stood.

"Attention on deck!" Sutton called, regret ringing in his voice.

The captain returned the papers to his briefcase and snapped it shut. "Carry on," he said.

LETHAJOY SUGGESTED THAT the "defense team" celebrate. Barney Pilcher accepted her offer of an early dinner at an Irish restaurant, perking up when she also offered to pay. Neal tried stifling a grin after they were seated but could not conceal his joy at what looked to be the death of the case against him.

"It isn't every day you dodge a bullet," Lethajoy said.

"Thanks to you," said Neal.

Barney looked up. "They're calling it a Christmas miracle at the legal center. Heard a couple of guys from the prosecutor's division in the head talking 'bout it. These guys I heard talking, they were pretty unflattering about you—"

"Junior," Lethajoy cut him off, "I take that as a compliment coming from prosecutors—the more of them I piss off, the better I like it." She placed a hand on Barney's sleeve. "They didn't want me anywhere near this. That's the whole reason they assigned you to defend. Figured Sutton could bully you, if not in the courtroom, then in the passageways later. I've seen him collar you. No offense, Barney, but you're still wet behind the ears, Gonzaga Law School or not. You were set up to lose this one."

Barney Pilcher lowered his head. "I've already been getting grief."

"How high?" Neal asked, his heart shifting to top gear as he pictured someone behind scenes pulling strings. "How high does this go? Who's behind it, Barney?"

"Whoa, Commander, I just meant about taking flak from other lawyers at the center."

Neal chided himself for imagining Barney knew anything. The young officer would be kept in the dark as much as possible. Hadn't Lethajoy just pointed out that Barney was the sacrificial lamb?

NEAL STOPPED THE MIATA just after pulling into the driveway at their Spanish Hills house. Close to midnight, hours later than he'd hoped. The drive through LA had been slowed by a police pursuit on the 405 and a pileup at its end. He'd had to keep the top down and the air on his face to keep himself awake.

He got out and stood by the car, taking a long look at the house. Like many other homes along the curving streets, it was Mediterranean style, with vaulted ceilings and arched windows, a stately appearance. In the single lighted window, Yvonne sat reading, waiting up for him. The case against him had been dealt a blow, and for that he could feel relief. But it wasn't over yet, not until the charges were completely dropped.

"Thatcher is recommending the charges be thrown out," he said inside the house, holding Yvonne in their greeting hug and allowing himself a grin.

"That's wonderful, honey!" A smile burst on her lips. "Does that mean it's over?" She stepped back from him and gazed into his eyes.

"It's a positive step. But it's still up to the local admiral to accept or reject Thatcher's report."

Yvonne's smile faded. "I thought this was going to be it."

Neal drew her back into his arms, nuzzling her hair. "Just have to wait for a decision. In the meantime, we've got lots of time we can spend together. Take a little trip to Santa Barbara if you like. We can look at the lights." Yvonne remained silent in his arms, head turned away. They stood that way for minutes.

THE NEXT MORNING, NEAL found three boxes marked XMAS in the garage rafters. He wrestled the boxes down the ladder to the garage floor and carried them into the kitchen.

"No, Neal," Yvonne said, halting him on seeing the boxes. "Not this year."

"Why not?" Neal asked. "This seems like the one Christmas we ought to hang a wreath."

Yvonne put down the knife she'd been chopping onion with and rinsed her hands at the sink. "Just doesn't feel like Christmas. Only the two of us. . . ."

He'd been fearing this. "You're thinking about having to drop the adoption plans, aren't you?" He lowered the boxes to the floor and went to her. Taking her hands, he said, "Listen, honey, just as soon as they officially drop the charges, I'll get my job back and we can take up where we left off. Just a bit of a delay, is all."

Yvonne twisted her mouth, eyes filling, voice quavering. "It's not that easy, Neal. We can't just rewind the tape like it never happened." She jerked her hands out of his, a defiant set to her mouth. She turned back to the cutting board, attacking the pile of onion slices, reducing them to pulp.

Neal stood limp in the center of the kitchen watching her shoulders rock with the movement of the knife and her pale blond hair swinging in jerky motions. He lifted the XMAS boxes and shouldered the door to the garage.

Dinner began in silence, without candles. Yvonne finally spoke. "I'm sorry for acting like a shrew."

"I know this has been hard for you," Neal answered softly.

"I was so focused on the adoption . . ."

Neal took her hand across the table. There was nothing he could say to reassure her. Unless all charges disappeared, Neal's trouble would come to light and would have to be addressed in their background profiles with the adoption agency.

"I was thinking that we could invite Martha Schneider for dinner, now she's alone," Neal offered, hoping the holiday could be saved from being a total bust.

"Martha stopped by to drop off a fruitcake. She was headed back to Norfolk to spend Christmas with her son's family," Yvonne said, standing to begin clearing the table.

The holidays had never mattered much to Neal and Yvonne since there were no children to spoil and neither was particularly religious. But now even the purely social aspects of it were gone. No company Christmas party this year. No use spending time with people who blamed Neal, at least partially, for the company's troubles.

They had both accepted that their union would produce no heirs, following Yvonne's ectopic pregnancy early in their marriage. The necessary surgery resulted in permanently damaged fallopian tubes. They had rationalized that the nomadic life of a sailor and a sailor's wife was not the best for children anyway. For Yvonne it was a reluctant acceptance, given her love of children, tempered by memories of her own rootless childhood. Neal stoically accepted it as the way things were and would be, but he recognized Yvonne's disappointment. He hadn't, however, fully understood its depth.

He could see it, now that he was forced into thinking about it, in the way she was drawn to children riding in shopping carts in line at the supermarket, her Saturday storytelling at the library, her desire to teach.

Their own families were sparse and scattered, the closest being Yvonne's younger sister, Madeline, who eked out a Spartan living in Seattle as a crafter, selling her small wooden carvings and assemblages at street fairs. After Neal's mom had died, Rich moved across the country to become a policeman in a small town in New York state, where Neal preferred his sibling would stay. The brothers would occasionally exchange birthday cards with terse inscriptions, but they had otherwise avoided contact.

THE ENVELOPE ARRIVED NEW Year's Eve. Orders to appear for trial January 10. "Son of a bitch!" Neal balled it up and threw the letter with all the force he could muster at the den wall, but the paper simply bounced to the carpet. The phone rang, startling him as he was picking up the letter and smoothing it out on his desk. He grabbed the receiver and slowly lowered himself into his desk chair.

"They ignored Thatcher's recommendation—cocksuckers are really being blatant," Lethajoy said.

"I know. Just got the orders. I guess it doesn't make sense to ask if they can do that. Any new ideas why?" Neal said, feeling defeat, the boulder rolling back down the mountain.

"I'm sure they can gin up a bunch of reasons, but they don't have to. Nothing says Thatcher's recommendation has to be accepted or even considered. The Article 32 investigation is pro forma. In this case they didn't get what they wanted so they are just ignoring the whole exercise. Can you be here on the fourth?"

"If the world hasn't stopped by then."

"Yeah. Happy Y2K, Neal."

THE TEARS AGAIN. ALWAYS the tears to begin with until Yvonne thought for a while and firmed up her resolve, figured out a plan. Neal had come to expect the tears as a device allowing her time to think, like a speaker saying "uh." He had developed enough sense to say nothing right away. And even later, to offer no solution until she asked what he thought. Still, she was a solid, pragmatic partner. She credited her aborted ballet career and lifelong limp with teaching her how to accept the way things were, make the best of it.

Neal had often thought if he'd had a say in the matter, Yvonne's inner strength notwithstanding, he'd change the human design, turn down the emotional rheostat in women and turn it off altogether in men. He hated the feeling of helplessness that came at these times. His navy job had been easy. He could intuit enemy plans and diversions once he knew their target. He'd been trained in threat analysis at Naval War College. The opposition's goal was usually pretty clear: to kick your ass to one extent or another. The

response always made sense: cover your own ass or hide it—
kick his. Understanding the enemy was easy—easier than
dealing with the anguish of someone you loved, someone
you slept with, someone on your side.

He employed his pacification tactic, one that had worked
before, and just held her until he could feel the tears had
stopped, the sobs diminished.

"Did you know this before? Is this why you asked on the
way back from Ojai what I'd do if you went to prison?" she
said, eyes red and swollen.

"Anything could happen . . . anything just did. Lethajoy
wants me there on Tuesday."

"What kind of sick game are they playing, Neal?" She
rubbed a tissue across her eyes.

"Somebody apparently wants my court-martial real bad.
Could be some nameless admiral somewhere who doesn't
know me or care about getting me, just wants to deal with
the issue. The brass can stay pretty well hidden if they want,
plenty of guys like Sutton to do the dirty work, pawns like
Hamby to sign the paperwork. The Pentagon's got to be
tired of all the negative news about the navy, and they need
to nail someone to prove the service won't tolerate misconduct. Guess I'm it." Neal's voice sounded weary in his own
ears.

CHAPTER TEN

Neal was always taken with the height and sweep of the San Diego Bay bridge. The clean shape, with no structure above the roadbed, made the crossing feel akin to flying. And now, riding in Lethajoy's Explorer, he could see the view from the graceful span. Heading west from San Diego, the bridge traced a straight, ascending path until nearing Coronado, where it made a right-hand curve before returning to earth. The blue-painted bridge offered a changing panorama that slid past the windshield.

"When we're with Vance, play dumb and observe, Neal. We may have to eat a little dirt, but we got to get her to serve it up first. And I *mean* play it totally neutral, none of those menacing stares. Don't even imagine it will work with her like with a sailor. She's got nothing at stake so she can afford to be a hard-ass."

"Are you sure talking to her is legal?" Neal asked.

"That's my point about not trying to intimidate her. All we're doing is asking for a statement, only what she's going to say on the stand. No coercion or threats. You probably shouldn't be along anyway, so be cool." Lethajoy held him in a warning gaze a moment longer than he felt was prudent on the bridge doing fifty-five.

"Will Sutton be the prosecutor?" Neal said, pointedly staring straight ahead, an example, he hoped, for the driver. *I'm driving next time.*

"I expect so; no point in them dirtying up anyone else. Damn, I *hope* so. Maybe he'll pull another 'Hamby' and trample procedural rules." Lethajoy gave a small chuckle.

Lethajoy negotiated the street maze past the bridge and drove along the golf course perimeter. High-rent territory, like most of the exclusive peninsula town, with views of the vast greensward and Glorietta Bay. Hotel Del Coronado dead ahead with the Coronado Shores high-rises to the left. The homes along Glorietta Boulevard were a mix of styles, like an architectural museum display. All had the lush patina of wealth, even those that would be considered modest in another venue.

They parked the Explorer along the street. Neal followed Lethajoy up the flagstone steps through a landscape dominated by bird-of-paradise and palmetto to the house at the top of a low rise. The building was unremarkable, showing a plain face to the street. The only notable feature in the expanse of dun stucco was an oversized bay window.

Angela Vance came to the front door in tan shorts and a tank top—no bra. Neal caught himself remembering how she looked naked on the bed in the old hotel. The smell of incense wafted from the open door as he and Lethajoy stood at the top of the flagstone steps.

"Ms. Beltower, Neal, come on in." Angela touched her hair with both hands. "Sorry, I didn't dress for the occasion. I've only been home a few days and trying to catch up on my writing schedule. I couldn't get anything done on the damn book tour. Anyway, I'm glad to meet you." She extended a hand to Lethajoy.

"New novel?" the lawyer asked.

"Yes. You'll be in it, Ms. Beltower."

"How exciting," Lethajoy answered without pause, her voice flat. "*The Wench Strikes Back*."

"Good title—I'll run it by my publisher. Actually, I *am* working on a sequel to *Navy Wench*. It's about this retired guy who gets called back into the navy for boinking a subordinate's wife."

Neal clenched his fists, tightened his jaw until his teeth squeaked and moved a half step forward until he felt the back of Lethajoy's hand lightly on his chest.

"Just joking, Neal," Angela said quickly. "I should have remembered you're the touchy type. Come on in, let me get you something to drink . . . juice, tea?"

While Angela went to the kitchen, they sat in the butter-yellow leather sofa near the bay window. A two-foot fake Christmas tree stood on a side table waiting to be returned to its carton until next December.

"That's exactly what I was talking about, Neal. Keep it under control or wait in the goddamned car," Lethajoy Beltower said in a stage whisper.

Impose calm, Neal thought, feeling a bit embarrassed. *Remember the mental lever, turn down the anger, slow the heartbeat.*

Angela landed lightly in the reclining chair facing them and drew her legs up under her. "OK, Neal, I'm sorry about my comment. I thought you had been joking about the court-martial until some Neanderthal in a cheap suit showed up at the door with a subpoena. Said he was a federal marshal—had a badge and everything. Who knew they'd take *Wench* so seriously? Surprising, even for a bunch of navy tight asses."

She leaned forward, drawing a somber face, speaking to Lethajoy. "Look, I know you think I'm some kind of merciless bitch, but it costs a fortune to live here and it takes forever to see any money from my publisher. I have to keep going on the promotion circuit long as I can. Readers forget you if you don't." Angela turned to Neal and lowered her eyes, then looked up at him, voice softening. "I didn't intend to hurt you."

Neal said nothing, gauging her sincerity, her half-apology, as the best he could hope for.

"Has anyone from the navy interviewed you yet? Have you made any statements?" Lethajoy broke the short silence.

"Someone named Sutton called. He said he wants to take a statement. He'll be here tomorrow."

"Ms. Vance, I want to know what you plan to tell Sutton, and how you'll testify about the contents of *Navy Wench*," said Lethajoy. "When the prosecutor asks you whether Allen Neil is Neal Olen, how will you answer?"

Angela paused then spoke slowly. "Am I supposed to be talking to you like this?"

"Don't worry about that. In fact, I want you to tell Lieutenant Commander Sutton that I was here and that we talked. Tell him everything you tell me. This is all part of what we missed because you weren't at the earlier hearing. As the accused, we have the right to see the evidence that may be used against Neal before the court-martial gets started."

"This is all so stupid," Angela declared, staring pointedly at Lethajoy as if the lawyer might agree and just make it all go away. "I guess you need to know how I write to understand what I wrote. I don't sit here making up characters—too much unnecessary work, particularly for minor roles. I find someone who is something like what I need and just, sort of, *appropriate* them, like a body snatcher. For example, if I need a short-order cook character, I think about who I know that would fit, more or less, the rough characteristics I have in mind. Then I give him a new name, touch up his background and personality and voilà: a fully formed short-order cook with a ready-made history and real-life traits."

"Do you always, say, switch a character's job along with the personality?"

"Well, in the book, Allen Neil's a character *based* on Neal. In this case I didn't need to switch because Neal was exactly what I was looking for: same physical type, same job in the navy, same cute ass. Sorry, but it is, don't you think?" She exaggerated a wink at Neal, who stared back blandly, suddenly understanding what *sex object* meant.

"I wouldn't know. What about Gillian Lorenz? Is she you?"

"Don't I wish. She's perfect—like Liz Taylor before she got fat. No, she's just a character I'd like to be. There's really no way to create a complete personality that isn't partly the author, at least emotionally. Who do you know as well as yourself, or your lover?"

"Well, anyway, it probably won't make a difference now that you're available as a witness to answer directly," said Lethajoy. "With your testimony the novel itself doesn't matter much; it's pretty much become moot as an evidentiary issue. The prosecutor is going to ask the key question, the real-life question—whether you had sex with Commander Olen."

"If you could call it that."

At the door Lethajoy thanked Angela, shook hands briefly and stepped outside. Angela leaned close to Neal. "I'm sorry about all this, Neal. Who knew?" she said in a whisper. "Be here tonight at nine. I just want to talk."

HE KNEW HE SHOULDN'T be here, parked in his Miata in the dark on Glorietta Boulevard. He'd just listen to what Angela had to say, nothing else that could be construed as witness tampering. He'd keep his emotions under control. Get the hell out quick as possible. Perhaps her conscience was bothering her and she didn't want to talk in front of Lethajoy. Angela hadn't seemed afraid to meet him alone, assuming that she'd be alone.

He tried to remember *that* weekend, how they had spent their time, how she had been. *In charge*—the description that stuck in his mind. She had talked nonstop, sure of herself, as they drove his Miata into the Laguna Mountains. He hated the way he had fallen under her spell.

The hotel, a leftover from the gold rush days, had floors that squeaked and thin interior walls, and the bed needed a fresh mattress—details that did not end up in the book. But the place qualified for historic landmark designation. He would have preferred something modern and comfortable, but Angela went for quaint and charming.

They'd shared the bed, breathed each other's breath, explored the variations that exist lover to lover, differences that drove their excitement. The air had taken on a fall chill and carried wood smoke from chimneys, adding atmosphere to the town and their adventure. Neal wondered what of his memory was real and what was based on *Navy Wench*.

> *Gillian bent across his chest and brought her mouth to his right side, kissing and nibbling the soft skin below his rib cage. The sensation drove his shaft to rigidity, as she knew it would. Allen's hand clenched her buttocks, the other buried in her hair as she walked her lips up his side, nuzzling. An involuntary twitch stiffened his body when he felt her tongue in the hair under his arm.*

She drew back. "Relax. I'm a pheromone junkie. It turns me on." She led his hand between her legs to the proof of her claim. Allen slid his fingers between wet folds, bringing a gasp from her throat. She swung her leg over him and took him inside her, moaning with the penetration. She pressed her open mouth violently against his, crushing his lips, teeth to teeth. He thrust his tongue into her mouth and explored the backs of her teeth, drew her tongue into his mouth. Allen arched his back and tried to pull her down. Instead, Gillian rose, pressing her palms against his chest, and rolled to the side on her hands and knees. "Come behind me." She lowered her shoulders and turned her head to the side like a feline in heat. Allen quickly opened her legs and accepted her invitation. Gillian tightened her vaginal muscles when he entered her the second time and began his slow rhythm. Grasping her thighs, he drove deeply into her.

Gillian quickly reached climax and was nearing the crest of a second when she felt Allen stiffen and explode inside her and strain to continue thrusting, face contorted.

When breathing had slowed and they lay side by side, he lazily traced the contours of her breast with his index finger. She shivered as bumps rose on her skin.

"That was incredible. I wish it could always be like that," he said.

Gillian turned her head, focusing on his profile. "I give lessons. Have your wife give me a call."

Just what I need, he thought, as he climbed the flagstone steps: *Angela's imagination read aloud in the courtroom. How could I sit through something like that?*

Angela answered the door dressed as before, tank top and shorts, barefoot, droopy red hair. No wisecracks like earlier for the lawyer's benefit, an emotionless face. He suspected it might be her real face. Was this the genuine Angela, the one who wasn't "on" for television interviews or book signings, or picking up men?

She kept a "once-lovers" distance between them as she delivered a martini rocks at arm's length to him on the couch. Some tiny fear was evident in her eyes. It also showed in her subdued voice, her careful words. She was too smart to imagine this meeting in any terms other than verging on dangerous. She'd shown no such reluctance to his nearness in Julian or later on the desert floor near Borrego Springs. Tonight, though, it gave Neal a small but certain satisfaction that his presence made her squirm.

She slid into her big chair, taking a quick sip of her own martini. "Neal, I had a visit from my ex yesterday. He told me what happened at the pretrial investigation. He's plenty pissed about it. Me, you, that dyke lawyer. We're all on his shit list." She shifted position in the chair, folding her legs beneath her. "They called him back to appear at the court-martial and that set him off in a rage. He's supposed to be testifying to something about you and the chain of command. I couldn't tell exactly. When he's had a couple drinks and starts yelling, you can't understand him."

Neal ran a hand across his jaw, felt the day's stubble. "They're trying to make a connection that I was his boss on the ship. They're trying to build a case that what you and I did could have affected crew on the ship."

"That's absurd. Can they do that?" She cocked her head slightly, which Neal took as her look of interest. He'd seen her do it on the Dagmar interview.

"Between your testimony and his, the adultery charge would stick."

Angela rose and moved a few paces toward the bay window. Gazing in the direction of the golf course and Glorietta Bay, she said, "Ken doesn't want to go through that crap again about my rejecting his name, wanting to get a part of my book money, the inference of domestic violence." She faced Neal. "Worries they'll come after him next. All worked up about it, not to mention jealous—acts like he caught us in bed."

Neal thought a moment. "But why would Hoopingartner be worried they'd come after him? He hasn't really done anything."

She made a face, rolling her eyes. "Who knows? Paranoia maybe. Anyway, from what he said, you ought to just plead guilty and skip the court-martial." Angela shook her head slowly, making her disgust obvious. "But he's too chicken-shit to suggest it to you himself—he's all brainwashed on the officer-enlisted thing. Ken wants me to convince you to do it, like I've got any control. The abusive son of a bitch wants a little humanitarian consideration. So he asks me. That's a laugh."

She picked up her martini, took a taste and set it back on the end table. She slid smoothly onto the couch and leaned toward Neal, a hint of conspiracy in her tone. "Still, you might consider it, Neal. He can get crazy. That's another reason I left the jerk."

"You tell the police he was here?"

"It was the first call I made. I should have saved the dime. City cops say he hasn't threatened me yet. Maybe it's my imagination."

"And we both know better than that." Neal was tiring of her talk as anger sharpened her tone.

"When we were in base housing, the goddamned security police never filed a report any of the times I called them. They just told me to spend the night with friends and allow him to cool off. One of the ignorant bastards even said,

'Don't get all heated up, little lady,' like it was PMS. So now, no records of the assaults. As far as the city cops are concerned, it never happened—no chance for a restraining order. If he kills me, they promise to spring into action." She drained the glass. "I'm going to hire private security. Big guys with guns."

"There's no excuse for Ken to hit you. None at all," Neal said, suddenly feeling a pang of sympathy for her, imagining that beautiful face bruised and bleeding.

She drew a slow breath, calming herself. Neal took her pause to speak. "If I were to confess, plead guilty to make him happy, that'd make life easier for you too, wouldn't it?" He spoke deliberately, measuring his words. "Ken might leave me alone, leave you alone, too. You could stay home, write more crap, screw up other lives. Real convenient, Angela, only one flaw: I'm not going to spend a year in prison for *your* goddamned convenience." Neal locked her in a stare, his fleeting empathy for her gone.

"I could make it worth your while, Neal," she said quickly, seductively, as though she had known that would be his answer.

"Don't make me laugh," he said. "At least, when you testify, my *dyke* lawyer can cross-examine. It may be a small chance, but it's the only chance I have. I confess to this, and I lose everything without a fight. A conviction will wipe me out."

Angela stood, leaning forward, and placed a hand on his arm. He forced himself to open his fists as she spoke. "You're going to make me go through this crap, aren't you . . . I mean with Ken coming after me, blood in his eye? You would want that on your conscience?"

He regarded her as he never had any woman he'd ever known—evil, vicious—ready to sacrifice him, thinking he was still fool enough for her to sucker with the promise of sex. Not anymore. "I would," he said, rising and making for the door.

Neal had nearly reached the street when the blow struck just below his shoulder blades, dropping him to the flagstone path, robbing his breath. He thrust his arm out and found a trouser cuff. He grabbed and jerked hard, felt the foot come up, saw the form of a man fall back into the bushes. Neal rolled to his side, kicked with all the power he could summon and drove his heel into the attacker's thigh. The effort threw Neal onto his back; a stabbing pain from the rough edge of the flagstone left him immobile for seconds. He could hear a grunt and hard shoes scraping on the stone. He looked up in time to see the Louisville Slugger come around again and catch his upraised fingers in a glancing blow an instant before the bat collided with his skull.

FROM SOMEWHERE DOWN THE hall he could hear the beep, beep of a heart monitor and muffled voices. Neal opened his eyes and found himself in a hospital room.

"We'll keep you overnight. Just as a precaution. You could have a concussion, but I don't think so." The doctor shined a penlight in Neal's eyes. "The pinky on your left hand and lower arm took most of the blow. Simple fracture. We got the finger immobilized. There's a pretty good contusion across your back, too, and scrapes on an elbow and knee. You're going to be sore for a while."

Now the face over his bed was Lethajoy's, coming out of the dead white, antiseptic atmosphere of the hospital. She looked drawn, worried, but managed a smile as she touched the bedsheet that covered Neal's shoulder. He could think of nothing to say to her after ignoring her instructions about keeping a distance from Angela. And in any case, his tongue had swollen and his dry lips stuck together. She poured a glass of water from a carafe and slipped one hand under his bandaged head. He peeled his lips apart and sipped at the glass she held for him.

"That was real amusing, Neal," she said, without a trace of amusement. "Why hire me if you're going to do it yourself? It's bad enough you went there, but now you've got two paramedics and five cops ready to testify that you were at 'the famous' Angela Vance's home and ended up in an altercation—which you clearly lost." She was letting him have it without quarter now that he had proven he was well enough to be chewed out. "No other bodies lying around in the bushes, so you must have come out the loser." She shook her head slowly. "How'm I going to defend you if I can't trust you to act like a good client?"

Neal touched the bandage covering his hairline and pushed himself up in the bed. The throbbing had begun in his splinted finger. "It was Hoopingartner," he said.

"And all this time I thought it was Mother Teresa. The cops want to have a little tête-à-tête about that in the morning. I called your wife. She's ready to drive down. I told her to wait to hear from you." She poked the number into her cell phone keypad and waited a few seconds. "He's here."

Neal took the phone. "Yvonne, I'm OK, just sore as hell."

"I'm sore as hell, too. What were you doing there?" Her voice carried concern and confusion.

Come out with it—your wife has a right to know, he told himself. "Angela . . . holding back on something, she wouldn't say in front of Lethajoy. Asked me to come back to talk. Tried to get me to plead guilty. I told her go to hell."

"So she threw you down the stairs?" Yvonne asked.

Neal convinced Yvonne to stay in Camarillo for the moment, to keep looking for a job. He was perfectly able to feel stupid without being reminded by seeing himself through her eyes. Lethajoy could take care of dropping the raft-load of recriminations on him now that he had gotten civilian police involved.

He looked up at Lethajoy, whose expression had softened. "I guess that was kind of dumb," he said.

LETHAJOY HAD HER FEET on her hatch-cover desk, eyes red from missed sleep, when he got to her office the morning after the bat attack. Aside from some dizziness when he got out of bed and feeling sore, Neal was able to drive to Lethajoy's building from the hospital. He gratefully accepted the coffee she poured from an old chrome percolator.

She waited for him to have a few sips. "The bat was in the bushes. They picked some of your skin and blood off it and they're running the fingerprints, though there isn't much doubt whose they are. Since both you and Angela saw him and his aggravated assault—or even attempted murder—your testimony along with the corroborating evidence will put him away, assuming they find him. If and when he gets out of state prison, the navy will probably take a whack at him for being AWOL. Hoopingartner could get time in the federal pen too."

"Maybe we'll be roommates," Neal offered glumly.

She swung her feet off the desk, a smile raising one side of her mouth. "There are definitely some joyful aspects to military law—and it isn't even double jeopardy—it's a whole new charge. A-W-O-L." Lethajoy held up the fax paper that bore the preliminary police report. "We have an 11:30 appointment with Coronado detectives. By the way, how did Hoopingartner know you'd be at Angela's?"

Neal considered for a moment. "Angela said Hoopingartner had been there the day before. Last night she had the drapes on that bay window open. If it was supposed to be an ambush, she could have signaled him when I didn't go along with their plan. But I can't be sure." He took a mouthful of coffee, swallowing slowly. "How will all this affect our case?" Neal leaned back in the chair. The slight pressure of the cushion across the purpling bat track just below his shoulder blades seemed to help the ache.

"Since you aren't dead they're going ahead with it. If they don't find Hoopingartner pretty quick, they can use the transcript from the pretrial investigation instead. There's the irony—he already had sworn testimony on record. It won't matter much whether he's there or not. The only difference is your injuries."

"I feel like I'm caught in a washing machine, getting batted from all sides."

"Lucky he didn't take your head off. Hoopingartner's latest wife would just as soon he stay on the lam. Word has it she's using the opportunity of his absence to make her own escape."

"According to Angela, he isn't any too fond of you, either," Neal said to the lawyer.

"Damn—I'm losing all my friends."

CHAPTER ELEVEN

The judge entered the courtroom wearing a humorless countenance and a black robe that concealed her navy uniform but not her ramrod bearing. Artificially jet-black hair hung straight except where she had pulled it back of her ears and clamped it down with barrettes. Captain Sandra Pickens sat down in the high-backed swivel chair behind the bench. She paused for an extended moment to scan the roomful of uniformed personnel and Lethajoy Beltower.

The cast for the arraignment was the same as it had been at the pretrial investigation, with the exception of Judge Pickens. The panel of five officers—four members and the president—detailed to sit in judgment would not be present. For the moment it would be legal housekeeping, certifying the qualifications of the judge and counsel. This would be Barney Pilcher's only opportunity to speak before the court. He grinned at the judge.

Lethajoy quickly stood. "The defense challenges the military judge with having a personal bias, Your Honor—"

"Perhaps defense would be so good as to explain its allegation," Pickens said quickly, knitting her eyebrows.

"Your Honor, surely you remember your part in forcing me to resign my commission."

"I do, Ms. Beltower, but not because of any bias as you allege, unless you are presuming to suggest that carrying out my duties under Navy Regulations and the Uniform Code of Military Justice is a matter of bias. Your challenge is denied."

Expected. Rehearsed. Delivered for maximum effect. An unpleasant surprise to Neal. He hadn't known about the connection between Lethajoy and the judge.

Beside Neal, Barney Pilcher whispered to no one in particular, "What did you expect?"

"Commander Neal Edward Olen, how do you plead?" Pickens raised her right hand a few inches above the bench. "Before receiving your pleas, I advise you that any motions to dismiss any charge or to grant other relief should be made at this time."

"The defense has the following motions, Your Honor," said Lethajoy. "Defense moves for dismissal for reason of defective charges, preferred and sworn by a petty officer with no knowledge of the case."

"Irrelevant. Motion denied."

"Defense moves for dismissal of all charges as was recommended by Captain Thatcher, Article 32 investigating officer." Lethajoy's motion for dismissal was standard, denial assured.

Pickens spoke, following rapidly. "Captain Thatcher, who is not a JAG officer, clearly did not comprehend the gravity of the charges. Denied."

"No shit," Barney commented under his breath.

Lethajoy pursed her lips and glanced down to her notes. "Defense moves for dismissal of all charges because of unlawful command influence over these proceedings."

"Denied. Got anything else, Ms. Beltower?" Pickens said.

"Suppression of eviden—"

"Denied."

"Continuance to prepare—"

"Denied. Now, Ms. Beltower, shall we get on to the pleas?"

Lethajoy touched Neal's shoulder and he rose stiffly, facing Judge Pickens, the movement shooting a bolt of pain across his back and causing his head to throb. Lethajoy spoke for him. "Commander Neal Edward Olen pleads not guilty to Article 133, Conduct Unbecoming an Officer and Gentleman, and not guilty to Article 134, Adultery."

"I'LL QUIT IF YOU want, Neal, if you think that I'm a liability to you." Lethajoy peered across the hatch-cover desk, arms and hands flat out before her like the Sphinx.

The thought had occurred to him, seeing the hostility of Judge Pickens toward Lethajoy. Would the judge's enmity slop over onto him? "I don't suppose she'd grant time to change counsel?"

"You see what she thinks about my motions, so I doubt it. Ol' Sandra was ready for me, like she'd been reading my notes. Canny old broad cut me off when I moved for a continuance for further preparation. I suppose we could try, but the panel members are going to be seated tomorrow, which makes her less likely to slow things down. It's pretty clear the navy just wants her to get through this thing. They're not worried about losing the appeal. It's the court-martial that counts and ends up on television news. That she gets to bounce me around for a couple of days is a bonus."

Neal felt a scowl form across his forehead. "What was that all about between you and the judge? I mean before today."

"She's the one who caught me and Susan being real friendly to each other, is all," Lethajoy said offhandedly, continuing, "Even if Pickens grants the time to swap counsel, you take the chance of not finding anyone willing to take the case on short notice, or at all. You're not much of an attraction for a defense attorney—it would be like being hired for a high dive into a wet sponge." Lethajoy leaned back, squeaking the chair. "The other thing you could do is go with Barney as lead counsel and me as ventriloquist. Gotta tell you, though, the kid scares me."

Neal looked across the lacquered expanse of old wood at his attorney, remembering why he had hired her in the first place, remembering the way Curtis Rassiter back in Camarillo had talked about her with grudging but real respect—and her claimed 90 percent success rate.

"Any chance to win, or is this one of the 10 percent losers?" he asked.

"Still possible either way."

"I don't suppose Pickens would have a convenient heart attack?" Neal asked, frustration growing.

"Two problems: One, a replacement judge would probably not be that much better. There's clearly plenty of pressure from the top to move this along smartly and not much sympathy for you." Lethajoy produced a tiny smile. "And two, Sandra Pickens has a heart that sets off airport metal detectors."

"THE SCHOOL INTERVIEWS WENT all right, but I'm not looking forward to all the crap outside the classroom," Yvonne said, her voice over the phone lacking enthusiasm. "I checked with the county adoption agency to see where we stood. They said if I wanted to reapply as a single person . . . they assumed that you were already in prison." Her voice went husky.

"This ought to be over with pretty quickly, sweetheart." He let his voice soften. Neal missed his wife more than ever, now that the court-martial had come before a jury. The main event would begin in the morning. But what could Yvonne do here in San Diego? She had forgiven him, but if the navy did not, he didn't want her here to hear the jury's pronouncement or to face the reporters.

Probably the best he could hope for was leniency in sentencing, a conviction without punishment, though that seemed unlikely since that was a big part of the reason they had come after him, to remedy the light punishment given to officers in the past.

He shook the thought from his mind and repositioned the phone close to his lips. "How are you holding up?" he asked.

"I'm thinking more about getting a dog," she said.

"Can we talk about it when I get home?" said Neal, who was allergic to dogs. "At least to figure out whether we can feed a pet, whether we'll have a place to keep one?" He was annoyed that this should come up now, when the future was so foggy. But maybe that was the very reason she wanted an animal—to hang on to as everything else collapsed around her.

"As long as you aren't just putting me off, Neal. I'm serious about this. And I don't want a house gecko!" She reminded him in mock seriousness of the delicate green lizards that were almost universally accepted, loved in Hawaiian homes, even by those like Yvonne who were generally skittish about such naked crawly creatures. The gecko earned his keep by staying out of the way and terrorizing insects.

Neal smiled, the first time this week. "OK, no geckos. I'll sniff around until I find an animal that doesn't make me sneeze. I hear llamas make good pets and can carry the groceries in from the car."

CHILDREN. AS CLOSE AS Neal had gotten to a child during his adult life was in the Kaiwi Channel keeping Kimo Puhoi's head above water while the ferry they had both been aboard minutes before turned to a reciprocal course. But that wasn't really being close, not like the rare moments when Neal's father had made him laugh or taught him to catch brook trout with nothing but patience and his hands. So long ago, before the bad times.

In the Kaiwi Channel water, Neal first heard the blast of the air horn, then caught sight of the ferry approaching as the two humans rode the heavy sea chop to a peak. But the ship plied a course that would have it pass by at least a half mile away. Neal swung the water-heavy white shirt he had taken off earlier over his head. After treading water and helping the child stay in the life ring for half an hour, it took all his strength to get the shirt out of the water with sufficient force to fly above his extended arm. He kept arcing it in the air, fatigue setting into his shoulder, until he could see the ship change course toward them.

"They're coming," Neal's voice was barely audible to himself, raspy and hoarse. He stole a glance at the child, seeing his eyes widen, the mouth open vainly to form a sound, maybe a word. "Won't be long now, Kimo."

In minutes two swimmers from the ferry were in the water with a pair of life jackets for the boy and his rescuer. The line they brought with them was tied to the flotation vests, and men on the ferry, now standing dead in the water, hauled them to the auto ramp and hoisted them aboard.

Hands came from all sides, wrapping the two in blankets. Voices of congratulations, crying. The sound of a helicopter arriving overhead.

Two men helped Neal to a chair on the main deck where he could see people bending over Kimo, stretched out on a blanket spread on the steel deck. The boy's hands flailed limply. He was alive and that was what counted.

"That's Kimo's mother." Neal looked up, trying to catch his breath, feeling congestion in his lungs, needing to cough out some seawater. Yvonne was pointing to a crying, keening Hawaiian woman straining against arms holding her back while an older man calmly checked Kimo's pulse and listened to his breathing. "Doctor on vacation," Yvonne said, kneeling beside her husband, clutching him to her breast, an expression of relief. "I was so afraid I'd lost you."

The man attending Kimo stood, smiling at the woman. She dropped to her knees beside her son and rocked him in her arms. That was enough for Neal. He closed his eyes.

"YOUR HONOR, MR. PRESIDENT and members of the court-martial panel," Merlin Sutton began in stentorian tones, too grand and loud for the modest size of the polished-oak courtroom. "The government will show that Commander Neal Edward Olen, a member of the fleet reserve, did, while on active duty, commit one or more acts of adultery and is guilty as well of conduct unbecoming an officer and gentleman."

The five officers serving as jury sat alert, watching Sutton. The panel was arranged with the senior member, a captain wearing the gold star of command on his uniform breast, in the center chair. Above his ribbons, a gold surface warfare badge. The opposite breast bore a black-and-white badge bearing the engraved name POSEY. He was characteristically trim, as were virtually all military men who had achieved command status, a physical fitness exemplar for the men and women under him. Captain Posey had the look and demeanor that would propel him to flag rank, barring a misstep along the way. In addition to competent command of his ship, the captain would need a sharp political acumen to carry him safely through the inevitable Pentagon assignment senior officers faced. His presence on the court-martial board was not a good sign for the defense.

"He's experienced the power," Lethajoy had whispered to Neal as Captain Posey took the center chair in the jury enclosure. Neal knew what she meant. As a ship's captain he had authority over his crew to adjudge guilt and award nonjudicial punishment at captain's mast. Aboard a large ship, that could amount to a weekly exercise of his power to punish infractions of the Uniform Code of Military Justice. Minor drug offenses, disrespect, unauthorized absences—all nature of petty crimes could be handled at captain's mast.

What concerned Neal was not so much the power Captain Posey possessed but the real possibility that, like a veteran cop, his view had hardened. In their navy careers, both Lethajoy and Neal had heard this presumption of guilt articulated as "If he ain't guilty, what's he doing standing in front of me, making up some cock-and-bull story?"

Neal sensed Barney beside him stiffen his posture. Perhaps even the kid sensed the real power Posey possessed. Barney leaned around behind Neal, whispering to Lethajoy, "You should have challenged the senior member in voir dire. He looks like an executioner."

They had accepted the panel as it had been initially constituted, for it appeared to be as representative as any other mix of officers they might achieve through the jury selection process. Lethajoy ignored Barney's after-the-fact suggestion. Nothing could be changed now.

The other four impaneled officers were arranged by rank alternately to Captain Posey's right and left—a lieutenant commander, two lieutenants and an ensign. Sutton faced the panel, knowing he need convince only four of them to achieve the two-thirds vote he had to have to convict. "The government will prove that the accused committed an act of moral turpitude and that this act constituted conduct unbecoming an officer and gentleman. Then you will have no choice but to find Commander Olen guilty and to impose the appropriate punishment, which may be dismissal from the service, forfeiture of all pay and allowances, and confinement for up to one year."

Sutton turned back to his table, glanced down at his notes while all eyes followed, waiting for the next point. He again faced the panel. "But gentlemen, you will *not* hear from Commander Olen, the accused. You will not because he has refused to take the stand, look you in the eye, and explain his actions. Thank you."

Judge Pickens swung her gaze toward Lethajoy. "Opening statement, Ms. Beltower?"

"Thank you, Your Honor." Lethajoy stood and began slowly, carefully scanning the faces of the officers seated behind the low partition of the jury box, giving them an opportunity to study her. Neal wondered if the panel had been quietly made aware of Lethajoy's earlier military service and the "dishonorable" reason for her leaving the navy—not that it seemed at all to be a secret within the legal center.

Sutton could arrange it to be known accidentally. It was easily the kind of thing one overhears in the men's head. It could happen anytime, could appear to be an innocent conversation about the lezzie lawyer between a couple of JAG officers taking a leak.

"Your Honor, members of the court-martial panel. The government will no doubt attempt to show you all that Lieutenant Commander Sutton mentions. I'll be interested in hearing that story as well because I cannot imagine why my client, a nationally known, bona fide navy hero, has been charged in what amounts to a show trial. Unless it is precisely *because* he is a nationally known, bona fide navy hero.

"We will show that the government, smarting from recent publicity about sexual misconduct in the ranks and out, is looking for someone to answer, a single scapegoat to carry away the sins of the many on his head.

"This case came about because of a best-selling novel called *Navy Wench*. And you can bet if the prosecutor forgets the fictional part of his case that I'll be sure to fill it in for him." The ensign on the panel gave a subdued but clearly audible chuckle. "The Article 32 investigating officer, a navy captain and the commanding officer of a ship, recommended dismissing—"

Judge Pickens broke in. "Irrelevant. The panel will disregard mention of the investigating officer's recommendation, and you will refrain from mentioning it again, Ms. Beltower. Reporter, strike Ms. Beltower's last sentence."

Getting slow in your old age, judge, Neal said to himself. *You should have seen that coming, Sandra.*

Lethajoy resumed, unfazed. "Commander Sutton decries my client's exercise of his right to not take the witness stand, but there is no requirement—it says so in Article 31 of the

UCMJ and in the Fifth Amendment of the U.S. Constitution. In fact, we do not intend to call any defense witnesses because, quite simply, there was no one to witness anything." Lethajoy took her chair.

"Trial counsel, you may begin your examination," Judge Pickens said.

Sutton rose. "Thank you, Your Honor. Prosecution calls Naval Criminal Investigative Service Special Agent Michael Godat."

Lethajoy leaned over and whispered to Neal, "You'd think he would'a learned."

The agent testified exactly as he had at the pretrial investigation with a mood of condescension that had not improved. Lethajoy cross-examined as she had before, pointing out the agent's casual methods—mostly watching television and reading *Navy Wench*.

"Agent Godat," Lethajoy said once she had him sufficiently pissed off and showing it, "at the Article 32 session the investigating officer asked you a few questions. According to the transcript," she held up a white binder, "when asked whether in your professional opinion there was a case against Commander Olen, you answered no. Is that correct?"

"I said it was the lawyer's job—" Godat began before the judge interrupted.

"Witness will not answer. Ms. Beltower, I instructed you to say nothing more about the pretrial investigation."

"Your Honor, my apologies. I understood you to prohibit mention of *Captain Thatcher's recommendation to dismiss.*"

Zing! Neal said to himself, *the girl's got balls*, knowing that she couldn't get away with too much of that with Judge Pickens—but the point was to let the jury hear the investigating officer's opinion.

"You remember wrong, counselor." Pickens glared.

"Yes, Your Honor. May I have clarification, please? Does that prohibition apply as well to the prosecution's intention to introduce sworn testimony from one Kenneth Hoopingartner from the pretrial investigation?"

Neal loved it, watching the way Lethajoy squared her shoulders and drew herself to her full height as she homed in on the judge's inconsistencies. He strained to keep a blank expression.

"I will rule on admissibility of the evidence at the appropriate time," Pickens responded, looking irritated at being caught in a discrepancy, but without raising her voice.

Lethajoy returned to the witness. "Let me rephrase my question: Agent Godat, based on your investigation, do you believe there is sufficient evidence to prefer charges?"

"Object! Your Honor, Agent Godat's job has nothing to do with making such decisions," Sutton burst out.

"Sustained. Stick to the witness's testimony of fact. No speculation." The judge was losing composure by degrees.

"I have no more questions," Lethajoy said, turning away from the witness.

Sutton leapt to his feet, agitated. "Agent Godat, do you stand behind the facts in your investigation report, and are they true to the best of your knowledge?"

"Yes, sir."

"No more questions, Your Honor," Sutton said, a smug set to his jaw.

Lethajoy stood. "I have a further question for the witness. Agent Godat, when did you inform Commander Olen of his rights?"

"That wasn't necessary since I never spoke with him directly," Godat answered quickly, on guard.

"Then do you know of anyone who informed him of his rights as the accused? The prosecutor or any other investigator?"

"No."

"No further questions, Your Honor." Lethajoy returned to the defense table.

As Godat walked out, clearly miffed, Sutton called Clarence Swain, the police officer who had shown up at Angela Vance's house following Hoopingartner's attack on Neal.

"I was dispatched to the location where I found an unconscious subject who appeared to have been mugged. The woman who had reported said the perpetrator looked to be her ex-husband, a . . ." Swain flipped his pocket notebook open, sounding out the syllables. "Kenneth Hoo-pin-gartner. After the attack he ran across the street to a dark-colored Toyota and drove off."

Lethajoy rose. "Officer, isn't a mugging a robbery? What was taken from the victim?"

"Nothing that I know of."

"So isn't it possible that rather than robbery being the motive, the attack could just as well have been assault— aggravated assault? Did Ms. Vance express any fear of her ex-husband, the man she had apparently just seen brutally beat Commander Olen with a baseball bat?"

"Well, she seemed excited but not scared."

"No further questions." Lethajoy walked away from the witness stand as the prosecutor rose.

Sutton had calmed. "At this point, Your Honor, I would call for the sworn testimony of Kenneth Hoopingartner from the Article 32 investigation be read into evidence —"

"Objection, Your Honor," Lethajoy interrupted.

"Your Honor," Sutton quickly responded, "this testimony is relevant and sworn and speaks directly to the relationship of Angela Vance and her ex-husband. This witness was, de facto, a subordinate of the accused. The investigation testimony establishes this fact."

Lethajoy stepped in quickly. "Your Honor, I will withdraw my objection if the entire transcript of the witness's earlier testimony, prosecution *and* defense, is read into the record."

"That was always my intention, Your Honor." Sutton pasted a solicitous smile on his face.

"Very well," said the judge. "Reporter, you will enter the entire Hoopingartner portion of the transcript into the record at this point and read the testimony aloud."

"Your Honor," Lethajoy said in an urgent tone, "I request that the tape of that testimony be played for the court so the panel can hear for themselves the actuality and the voice of the witness. I checked and found the tape is available." She cast a coquettish glance at Sutton.

Pickens considered for moment. "I'll allow it. Recess for fifteen minutes while the tape is set up."

Neal leaned toward his lawyer, eyebrows raised. Barney also craned to hear. "Why?"

"It shows the kind of people we're dealing with. Brings in the question of credibility."

As HOOPINGARTNER'S RECORDED testimony ended, Lethajoy nodded toward the jury box and whispered to Neal, "They're about as expressive as Mount Rushmore; can't tell what they're thinking."

"Should have challenged Captain Posey at voir dire," Barney reiterated.

Merlin Sutton stood and said, "Call Angela Vance." The timbre of his voice was as if he were announcing a head of state.

Neal tensed, hearing her name. After he had turned down her proposal that he confess, he had no idea what she'd say. Was she behind the bat attack, in it with Hoopingartner?

Angela made her entrance. She was wearing a pink suit with a maroon silk blouse. Her hair was fluffed, shimmering in the light. In spite of her dramatic attire she looked subdued, nervous, not at all like her television appearances. He knew there'd be no trademark cackle from her today. He could not identify what all he was feeling watching her. There was the elation that any man would experience on encountering a knockout woman, but his dominant emotion was anger—anger with her but mostly with himself.

Angela returned Neal's gaze as she passed the defense table, giving nothing away, as if they were strangers passing in the street.

Barney took in a quick breath. Neal knew what the junior officer was thinking—what any male with a full load of hormones would.

Lethajoy leaned close to Neal, speaking softly. "She's not so perfect. A redhead in pink and maroon—makes her look washed out."

"Ms. Vance, when and how did you come to know the accused?" Sutton began.

"I met him in the Old Tijuana Restaurant bar. It must have been near the end of 1995."

Just like the goddamned book, Neal said to himself, tensing, *just like it happened*. Lethajoy, without taking her eyes off Angela, lightly touched Neal's sleeve, her signal to relax that she had been employing increasingly now that they were in court where his demeanor mattered.

"Was this a casual meeting?" Sutton asked.

"It was a pickup."

"By 'pickup' you mean that Commander Olen initiated the contact?"

"Nobody picks me up. It's always the other way around if it's going to be at all." Angela's voice carried a tone of defiance.

"After that, your new relationship with the accused went beyond dinner?"

"Yes." She crossed her legs demurely.

"Without going into intimate detail, please tell how this relationship progressed."

She answered matter-of-factly. "We met on a Friday. The next day we took a drive to Julian and stayed in a hotel there. The day after that we drove down to the desert— Borrego Springs area. We got back to Coronado Sunday evening. That was it."

"Then Commander Olen broke off the relationship?"

Angela looked mildly exasperated. "The other way 'round. I picked him up and I dropped him."

"Why?"

"He was all doe-eyed, but I could see I was making him nervous."

"The hotel where you stayed in Julian, ah . . . did you share a room?"

"That was the whole idea. That's probably what made him nervous."

"And it was in that hotel room in Julian that you had your first sexual encounter with the accused?"

"Yes." Angela spoke almost defiantly, failing to disguise a growing disdain for her questioner.

Shit, Neal said to himself. *She might as well go home now. That's all Sutton needs to bury me.* He felt his cheeks reddening with anger and embarrassment.

"And you had a second sexual encounter. Was that at the same hotel?"

"No."

"Why was that?"

"It was an old building."

"I don't understand."

"Old building, old bed, thin walls—everything squeaked. You could hear applause from the next room when we finished."

Neal sensed the jurors' eyes on him. A few chuckles intruded on the courtroom atmosphere.

"When and where did the second sexual encounter occur?"

"The second *sexual encounter*"—she spat her answer— "was the next day, Sunday, behind a sand dune in the desert."

"That seems like an odd place for sex."

Angela revealed exasperation. "Read the book. It *was* odd sex. That's the whole point, isn't it?"

"I don't understand," Sutton said.

"I don't imagine *you* would," Angela responded.

"Keep your opinions to yourself, Ms. Vance!" Judge Pickens said, hiding a smile.

"At that time, in 1995, were you married?" continued Sutton.

"Yes, to Kenneth Hoopingartner."

"Kenneth Hoopingartner is a suspect in a nighttime attack on the accused outside your home. You saw the attack and called 911. Is that right?"

"Yes."

"How did Commander Olen come to be at your home?"

"He was there during the day with his lawyer. I asked him to come back alone. I wanted to talk to him."

"About what? And are you sure it was just talk? Did you have romantic intentions?"

"If you're talking about more *sexual encounters*, definitely not. I wanted to tell him how sorry I was about all this mess as a result of my book, you know, just to ask him to forgive me. Bury the hatchet, have a drink. I didn't want to do that with his lawyer there."

"What else did you talk about?"

Angela hesitated, then lowered her head and her voice. "He said . . ."

"Please speak up, Ms. Vance," Judge Pickens urged.

"He didn't want me to testify. I said I had to. According to the subpoena I could get six months in jail if I blew it off. He got mad and left. That's when he got attacked."

Neal leaned toward Lethajoy. "That's a lie," he whispered. He could feel his face get hot again with anger.

Lethajoy placed a hand on his arm, whispering, "Listen."

Sutton turned toward the judge. "Your Honor, prosecution moves for preferral of the additional charge of Article 134, Paragraph 96, obstructing justice."

"Counsel, approach the bench."

Sutton and Lethajoy stood close before the judge. Neal couldn't make out the *sotto voce* argument. The two returned and Lethajoy sat staring straight at Pickens until the judge spoke again to the courtroom.

"Motion denied. You'll need more than that, Commander Sutton." Judge Pickens spoke in a flat tone, clearly unhappy about having no choice but to find for the defense.

Lethajoy leaned close to Neal, speaking quietly. "Merlin tried stretching that charge to fit, but it's still just he-said, she-said."

Sutton turned to Lethajoy wearing a blank look. "Your witness, counselor."

"We'll reconvene tomorrow at zero nine hundred." Judge Pickens began stacking the papers spread before her.

Lethajoy was already on her feet. "If it pleases the court, it's only fifteen thirty. Defense requests an opportunity to begin questioning the witness while prosecution's examination of Ms. Vance is still fresh in the panel's mind."

"Can you complete your questioning before 1600?"

"No, Your Honor, but I can begin today and take up again tomorrow."

"Request denied. The panel has been here all day and, unlike you, Ms. Beltower, these are still active duty officers with responsibilities outside their additional service to this court. I cannot in good conscience needlessly extend the time they are here."

"Your Honor—"

The only answer was a gavel tap and the rustle of Judge Pickens's robe.

IN THE PASSAGEWAY, ANGELA Vance, surrounded by reporters and unrestrained by courtroom decorum, loudly pitched her book. Merlin Sutton was giving hurried instructions to a yeoman when Lethajoy, Neal and Barney emerged from Judge Pickens's domain. Sutton turned to the three. "Why not argue your First Amendment right to bore the bejesus out of everybody, counselor? Couldn't you see the panel was starting to nod off?" Sutton laughed and flicked a hand at the enlisted man, who pulled a chagrined look and wandered away.

"Merlin, it was during *your* examination of a gorgeous woman that the jury went to sleep. That's real talent. You're like a dose of Valium."

A reporter's microphone suddenly thrust between Lethajoy Beltower and Merlin Sutton. Lethajoy regarded the woman holding the mike, then pointedly ignored her while speaking up. "I thought legal center policy was to allow in only one pool reporter, Merlin, or is this gathering something special you cooked up for my client?"

Several more reporters came near, abandoning Angela Vance. A video camera light came on. The reporters sensed the greater drama in two lawyers sparring outside the courtroom. Neal tried to stand back from the light, and Barney had disappeared somewhere.

The gathering crowd stood, without their usual babble of questions, waiting for the two antagonists to resume. The silence continued for long seconds as Lethajoy stared at Sutton, chin thrust forward, ignoring the crush that now packed the passageway around them.

"Ms. Beltower," Sutton spoke to her slowly and with enough volume to allow clear audio recordings, "I'm sure that you understand that we are merely extending a courtesy to our media friends, allowing them to wait inside the building, and to speak with Ms. Vance, a famous personality. In case you hadn't noticed, it's January and cold out there. Of course that's uncommon for San Diego." He now faced the reporters with a chuckle. "Please don't tell the Chamber of Commerce I said that." No one laughed.

Lethajoy pushed through the crowd, clearly realizing that she could not improve on the impression Merlin had on the reporters all on his own. She led the way with Neal close behind. The throng around Merlin Sutton dissolved; reporters followed them outside to the edge of the quay wall, where Lethajoy turned to face them with a serene smile, a harbor tug idling in the background. The smell of marine-grade diesel exhaust hung in the cold, still air. Neal noticed Barney hurrying out of the center to join them.

"Was it just me or did you notice it was getting stuffy in

there? Thank you for coming out, in spite of the *frigid* San Diego weather—and *pul-eeze* don't tell the mayor I said that."

A laugh arose from the group. "What's your strategy?" a voice called.

"Winning," she said.

"What do you think of *Navy Wench*?"

"I'd love to have one. Thank you all, but we have to go." Like a mother duck, she led Neal and Barney off through the group of reporters to her Explorer.

CHAPTER TWELVE

Neal and Barney joined Lethajoy in her office and ordered in pizza while waiting for the local newscast. She wanted to judge what the news shows would make of her name-calling match with Merlin. "I wish it hadn't happened," Lethajoy said after swallowing the last bit of a pizza slice. "I don't like to talk to the media too soon—especially in the middle of a personal pissing contest with the prosecutor. After the verdict is best, so we can avoid having to eat a prediction. Still, it was kind of fun to go at Merlin. The putz."

"You ought to get him on the soccer field," Neal commented, laughing nervously, not really in the conversation. Something was growing in a corner of his brain that had been nagging at him since it became clear that he faced a court-martial. He still found it difficult to accept that this was happening to him and he tried to blank it out, but he'd had too much practice at logic and realism. He had no choice but to face it. His mind drifted back to Hawaii, when Admiral Ellison had given him his "hero" assignment, speaking to local groups and schools, recruiting. A word he

151

had used a lot in his talks was "honor." Honor was easy until it came up against the urge for personal survival.

"Here it is." Lethajoy straightened in her chair and leaned toward the television.

An official navy portrait of Neal from his service record appeared behind the news anchorman. "In the court-martial of Commander Neal Olen today, defense attorney Lethajoy Beltower, an openly gay lawyer specializing in military law, spoke with reporters for the first time."

Video images began with the jerky pursuit of Neal and Lethajoy in the legal center passageway, then cut to a close-up of her standing on the quay wall. Then a shot of Angela facing a lone microphone; in the background, in the emptied passageway, Merlin Sutton and Barney Pilcher in animated conversation. Neal turned to stare at Barney now. The lawyer was busy pulling off another slice of pizza from the pie.

"Commander Olen, recognized as a hero by the president during his State of the Union address, is being tried for adultery, a crime in the military," the anchor continued. "The star witness in the trial is the best-selling author of *Navy Wench*, Angela Vance."

A new graphic appeared behind the anchorman, changing the subject, illustrating a story about illegal immigrants.

"Fifteen seconds," Barney said. "Five of that for Angela's book. Impressive journalistic depth, but they seem to like you—at least they didn't go out of their way to trash you."

Barney had played his role perfectly today, managing to keep pretty much quiet, his presence during the trial vague, like a specter. Neal knew the young lawyer had been seated at the defense table next to him but, except for his few mumbled comments, couldn't remember an awareness of him until they'd left the building. Barney hadn't been with them. The images in the news story explained why.

Lethajoy snapped off the television, speaking to Neal directly. "Looks to me like Barney here understands the navy way pretty well. He hasn't forgotten that after you and I are gone, he's got to live there, gets to see Merlin in the passageway every day. Isn't that right, Barney? That why you stayed behind today? Making plans for your future?" She faced him squarely.

"Is that some kind of an accusation?" Pilcher straightened.

Neal glanced at Lethajoy, then joined her line. "Pretty clear from that news video that you're consulting with the other side. What did Merlin, or was it Captain Watembach, tell you that you were supposed to do for me—or was it *to* me? Are you reporting back to Watembach what we say? Did he give you a Judas assignment, Barney?"

Lethajoy jumped in, waggling a piece of pizza at the young officer. "It would explain how Judge Pickens seems to know what I'm going to say before I say it. Sure would account for her prescience."

"This is bullshit," Barney countered, attempting a casual denial. But his shoulders tensed.

Lethajoy continued. "It would also explain why she was caught off guard by my Article 32 argument that Thatcher's recommendation be considered. We'd never discussed that so you couldn't have known about it."

"I can't believe you expect to prove any of this." Barney's eyes were downcast, refusing to meet Neal's or Lethajoy's.

Neal raised his hand, the splint and gauze wrapping immobilizing his broken finger like a traffic cop's white glove, a signal to stop. "No need to prove anything to fire your ass, Barney. I can do it because I lack confidence in your ability, but I'd say we've got reasonable suspicion that it's something else."

Lethajoy came around the desk and looked down on the junior officer. "I can understand how you might not be inclined to put yourself out on this case. You'd be expected to lose it as lead counsel. Why else would Watembach appoint a neophyte in the first place except to lose? Who could blame a new lawyer up against a fifteen-year veteran like Lieutenant Commander Merlin Sutton?"

Neal added, "And when you weren't lead counsel, couldn't blow the case on your own, you tried to sink the defense anyway. The way it looks to me."

"But how far are you willing to go to keep Merlin happy? How far can we trust the lawyer-client privilege if you're worried about your future in the JAG Corps?" Lethajoy asked.

Barney spoke slowly, incredulity sharpening his tone. "How can you question me like that? I'm really surprised. Do you think I'd just throw away my ethics to get along? That's insulting!" His voice rose. "I brought *you* information that I overheard, didn't I? Remember at the restaurant that time—about what they thought of Lethajoy, about the pressure from above?"

"That's not much of a giveaway, Barney—you could have read that much off the outhouse walls," Lethajoy said with a quiet intensity. "It's nothing we didn't already know. You forget that I lived in that snake pit, junior. Shit, I know all the snakes personally. You haven't convinced me that you didn't pass our strategy along."

Neal stood. "Time for you to leave, Barney."

Barney Pilcher didn't move from the chair.

"I'm not too old to throw your ass out that fucking window." Neal moved in tighter.

Barney maintained his silence as he got up and stepped a pace toward the door. "You're going in the tank regardless, *sir*," he said, then passed through to the hall, giving the door a firm shove behind him.

Neal drew a breath, letting the adrenaline subside. He had been prepared for action. He walked to the window and stood watching as Barney appeared below, walking briskly across the street.

"That sounded like a confession to me, Neal. Looks like we were right about the kid. The first rule of military lawyers is don't foul your nest," she said. "Makes me sick that he sold out on his first big case."

"I don't suppose it would do any good to complain."

"Any ideas about who might give a shit? We'd have to put the whole system on trial—sue the navy, the U.S. government. You ready for that exercise?"

Neal let the question roll through his mind. His first instinct was to wrap himself in principle and do battle. But he knew better—that fighting for a principle, no matter how noble, was most often a loser.

"Wanna talk about it?" The lawyer's voice had ratcheted down, become soft and conciliatory.

Neal looked up to see Lethajoy eyeing him as she would a troubled teenager. He dropped heavily into a chair.

"Let me guess," she said. "You're feeling like an outsider. Bet it's the first time. It's a shock when you find out that the navy isn't the snug little place you thought it was. It can get real impersonal real fast when they decide you're the bad guy."

"I guess you'd know about that," he said. "I mean—"

Lethajoy held up a hand. "It's a major fucking epiphany when you realize you've been kidding yourself, when you find out loyalty means nothing because it's a one-way street."

"So why'd you join, knowing you were on the shit list from the beginning?"

Lethajoy laughed. "I was Daddy's girl and grew up around the navy. He was a chief petty officer, so . . ." She turned her head away, gazing out the window. "Sounds pathetically naïve saying it now, but I thought I could make a difference, maybe get some changes made to the UCMJ. And, I have to admit, having the navy pay for college was a pretty good draw. I guess that we're even on that score—I gave them the six years in uniform that they wanted in return."

Neal felt as low as he ever had. "So what do I do now?"

Lethajoy refocused on Neal. "There are two ways you can go. Keep your mouth shut and let this thing play out, or short-circuit the show with a confession."

WHAT COULD THEY DO that would affect the court-martial's outcome? Neal opened the refrigerator in his Visiting Officers' Quarters suite and let his hand drift over the soft drinks, hesitating, then clutching a beer can. *No point in pursuing Barney no matter how I'd like to throttle the bastard,* he told himself, thankful he needn't worry about having a spy in his camp any longer. Lethajoy was right. Without solid proof, any complaint against the young lawyer could blow up in their faces. Just fire him, take him off the case and forget it, Lethajoy had counseled. Barney hadn't been much help, even in minor ways. Let the junior lieutenant make his explanation to his boss about why he was no longer at the defense table.

"I was tired of feeding him anyway," Lethajoy had commented earlier in the office as she folded the empty pizza box and pushed it into an already-full wastebasket. "Didn't once pop for dinner. Ate like an ox."

Now, as Neal pulled the ring on top of the beer can, a knock sounded at the door. "Yes?"

"Commander Olen, this is base security. Can you open the door? We need to talk to you about Hoopingartner."

Neal put down the beer, crossed the room and turned the lock. The door burst in, banging into the wall, driving him back into the room. Neal regained his balance as Kenneth Hoopingartner appeared in the doorway holding a small black revolver. Neal charged the man and took the heel of the pistol grip across his cheekbone. He saw explosions of light as he hit the floor.

Taking a further step inside, Hoopingartner pushed the door shut behind him and landed a kick to Neal's thigh. "Get up."

Neal got his right arm beneath him and rose slowly from the floor.

"Get up, motherfucker!"

Neal made it to his knees, then to his feet, and faced his attacker. He held his hand to his thigh, then took it away as the pressure of his touch intensified the pain. He assessed his chance of surviving this encounter as slim—too disabled to put up a fight and outgunned one to zero. This could get a lot more serious than a baseball bat attack. He looked for a weapon but nothing was near, nothing he could reach faster than Hoopingartner could fire the revolver.

"Get over there. Siddown!" Hoopingartner motioned with the gun.

Determined, grim, Neal crossed the room to the couch. He sat, holding the bandaged left hand that had been injured in his last encounter with Ken Hoopingartner. The door had struck his right shoulder, driving a wavering numbness through flesh and bone. He felt a trickle of blood from his cheek.

"Get out of here, Ken—you're in enough trouble already. The cops are looking for you." He spoke to the petty officer as though they were still aboard ship, as if the large man holding the small gun was somehow still a subordinate. It was the only reaction Neal had—to give an order and expect obedience. It was worth a try.

"I'm going to show you trouble, you son of a bitch. You can't screw my wife and get away with it so easy. I know about how you zeros get off. A little slap on the hand, a little pat on the ass. Meanwhile you and that bitch try to make me out some kind of psycho," Hoopingartner said, ignoring the irony.

"You're not helping yourself. Come on, think about this." Neal's mind raced, searching for something that would quell Hoopingartner's anger, something that would buy time until . . . *until he decides to put a bullet through my heart.*

"Shaddup! Just shut the fuck up." Hoopingartner wore jeans and a blue sweatshirt that, even with its loose bulk, failed to hide his well-developed chest and arms. A clean hit with the bat the other night would have splattered Neal's brains all over Angela's sidewalk. Making a second try tonight could only mean Hoopingartner had gone over the edge, lost his fear of capture—or was driven because of it. Neal's mind flashed on a principle he'd developed over the years in the intelligence game: You can't outsmart an idiot or a psycho. Unconventional thought, illogic, defied prediction. Saddam Hussein and Slobodan Milosevic were sufficient evidence that his belief was correct. Who could sanely predict that either would risk unwinnable war with the United States and its allies? Yet each ignored the obvious.

And each survived the allied onslaught.

"I didn't know Angela was married to you. How could I know that? She never said anything. Different name. . . ."

Hoopingartner roared, kicking the coffee table, sending it tumbling over. "Had to say it, had to bring it up."

Neal grimaced. "How could I know that's so important to you?"

"Like the rest of those assholes all my life makin' fun . . . hoop-de-doo, hoopin' crane, hula hoop." Hoopingartner squeezed his eyes shut for a second, then wiped a forearm across his face where rivulets of sweat had formed tracks.

A deep, shuddering breath preceded a change of tone, a softening of his voice, as he retreated into his own agonized memory. "Mister Jorgenson . . . seventh grade . . . called me *hoopskirt*. Hoopskirt, fer chrissakes. Son of a bitch thought it was funny, then gave me a ration of shit because I wouldn't laugh—laugh at my own name! Tol' me to relax—lighten up. I coulda killed that bastard on the spot." He stared at Neal, waving the revolver. A lightness crossed his face at the mention of a homicide too long deferred. A smile came like a quickly passing shaft of sunlight, immediately overtaken by the cloudy maelstrom of his anger. "How could I tell Mom and Dad their name wasn't good enough for my wife? Too long, too funny, she said . . . rather be Vance. Just go fuck yourself, *Hoopingartner*—my wife!"

Petty Officer Kenneth Hoopingartner moved to the recliner, keeping the revolver trained on Neal, and sat heavily in the chair, seeming fatigued from his exertions, his anger, from being on the run. He put a hand to his brow. "I don't know what I'm doing, Commander. Nothin's left. Got no place to go."

Seconds passed. Testing his right arm, Neal shifted on the couch, trying to draw himself up from an unbalanced sprawl. The revolver stared at him, following as his position and perspective changed slightly.

"Kenneth . . . Ken, I always treated you with respect. You may have another beef with me but not over your name."

No response. Hoopingartner looked past Neal, through him.

"Is that what this is all about, Ken, your name, about your seventh-grade teacher, cruel children, Angela? Even if it's been eating at you all this time, is it worth ruining the rest of your life?"

Kenneth rested elbows on knees and lowered his head, looking at the carpet between his shoes.

Neal pushed himself up a few more inches on the couch. "Something else, Ken. What is it? We can get someone to help you, whatever it is. Talk to me, Ken."

"I . . . I can't." He raised the revolver. Neal tensed, but Hoopingartner turned the barrel to the side and dragged his sleeve across his eyes. Wetness smeared on his cheek. "I heard the NCIS agent, that Godat guy, when I was waiting to testify. The door to the hearing room was open a little. Heard him, about the leak . . . about Keyhole."

The national surveillance satellites. Neal thought a moment, then said, "Godat didn't say it was specifically Keyhole, only that Washington was investigating a possible compromise."

"I told Angela about it. She put it in the book."

"OK, so you thought you'd impress her with a little pillow talk," Neal said, attempting to sound offhanded as he drew a long breath. For his twenty years as an intelligence officer he had protected classified information, and reconnaissance satellite programs had been top secret for thirty years. More than top secret—they were all protected with carefully limited "code word" access.

"That was a stupid move, Ken, just on general principles, but you're probably fine. Keyhole was declassified in '95; only the schedule is still a secret."

Ken's voice flat, eyes downcast. "It was before '95 I told her."

"That isn't the only thing you told her, is it?" Neal said, suddenly understanding that Keyhole was only the beginning, that there was more Ken had revealed that had still been classified. And it made no difference whether it was in the book or not, or that he had told his wife rather than China or Iraq. The government made no allowances for uncleared wives.

Neal realized that he was about to be shot by a traitor. "Did it work, Ken? Was she impressed?" Now Neal was getting pissed, imagining how he might launch himself across the coffee table, how he would take down this pathetic guy who'd break his oath to his country and sell out his honor for a piece of ass.

Tears had begun seeping from Petty Officer Kenneth Hoopingartner's eyes. His slump deepened. He lifted the .32 to his head, touching the barrel to the sweaty skin of his temple.

"Don't do it, Ken!" Neal yelled.

For the second time this night Neal's door burst open. The two men in dark blue uniforms were only a glimpse of movement. Startled, Ken dropped his hand and twisted toward the door behind him. A shot. Neal watched smoke issue in a lazy cloud from the short-barreled revolver in Hoopingartner's hand. The .32-caliber slug passed through Neal's right side above his belt line. He tried to roll away on the couch but felt like an upended turtle trying to rise from his back, trying to find purchase with his feet, to push off the cushion with his injured hand, slipping back. More shots from the doorway, smoke, shouting.

Now silent. Now dark.

"I SEE YOU FIGURED out how to get a continuance, Neal," Lethajoy said as she approached the couch where Neal was propped in front of the television in his reassigned Visiting Officers' Quarters suite. "If I'd thought of it I'da shot you myself."

"Just a flesh wound, as they say in the westerns," Neal responded. "No bones broken, and it missed all of the vital organs. I've got to hand it to Hoopingartner. He shot for minimum damage."

Yvonne had driven down from Camarillo immediately and was at the hospital by the time Neal had come out of anesthesia. Now, three days later, she'd brought him back to the VOQ and hovered around him as if afraid of the next possible melee.

Lethajoy accepted the soft drink Yvonne offered. "In no time at all we can get rolling on the court-martial again. I talked to the judge last night. Got her on the phone at home after a few drinks while her fangs were retracted. She's going to call the doctors to figure out how soon we can reconvene. Probably a week or ten days. Don't make any plans for Martin Luther King Day."

"I can't wait." Neal's mind snagged bits of remembered conversation from the night of the shootout. He felt sure he could piece it together, but he asked anyway. "Nobody's said what happened to Kenneth."

"He's dead, Neal. Took six slugs in the upper body. The guy in the room next to yours heard the noise—door slamming, raised voices—and called base police. They saw Hoopingartner's car in the lot. Lousy parking job, matched the all-points bulletin. They went in ready to do some blasting.

"Funny thing is that both these guys knew Hoopingartner. They'd been to his quarters when he went after his current wife. One of 'em even remembers him and Angela from back before they split up. He claims to be 'Officer Dick Head' from the book—thinks it's funny.

"You'll like this. When I got there, Officer Dick Head was writing a parking ticket for Hoopingartner's car—the guy he'd just smoked. This is while he waited for the detectives and the coroner to show up. Unbelievable." She shrugged. "Enlisted man's car in officer parking—what else could he do?"

"Cuff 'im?" Neal offered lamely, ready for more sleep, ready to forget everything but still feeling a need to talk. "Hoopingartner admitted to telling Angela about Keyhole satellites."

Yvonne leaned forward. "I never heard you talk about any Keyhole satellite."

"I couldn't discuss it before, but now it's been declassified," Neal said.

Yvonne, sounding just a bit hurt, said, "You never mentioned it to me." Like many military spouses she understood why her husband couldn't reveal classified information to her, but she'd still made it clear she felt left out, as though she personally couldn't be trusted.

"Habit," Neal answered. But now he told how the early Corona Project satellites imaged on film, which, incredibly, was ejected from an orbit a hundred miles above the earth. As the canister, containing over thirty thousand feet of film, plummeted to earth, slowed by a parachute, it was snatched midair by a specially configured U.S. Air Force plane. The later Keyhole Class surveillance satellite models used electronic imaging—eliminating the need for the complex and dangerous game of catch the canister.

"I saw a movie once where satellites could read the number off a telephone," Lethajoy said.

"That was science fiction," Neal said. "The maximum image resolution has improved over the years from six feet to about five inches. But they can now pick out a squirrel on the ground from two hundred miles overhead."

"Anyway," Lethajoy said, businesslike, "there could be a civilian inquest *and* a navy JAG investigation into Hoopingartner's death. Nothing for you to worry about, for a change. Pretty clear that you were an unwilling participant in that little battle—the only one without artillery."

"He wouldn't have shot me if they hadn't broken in. He was ready to shoot himself. Ken was starting to talk, like he just wanted to unwind a little. He confessed that he had told Angela about the Keyhole satellite and seemed about to tell me more," Neal said.

"And he actually figured that killing you would take the heat off him?" Lethajoy shook her head.

"Incredible, but it probably would have, at least for spilling secrets," Neal answered. "He wasn't thinking all that well. What he told Angela that ended up in the book has been declassified, he just told it to her too early. None of this would have come up if it weren't for *Navy Wench* and the adultery charge against me. He would have gotten away clean."

"But if it comes up as a charge against you, you wouldn't be believed that Hoop confessed to you just before he was killed. Sounds too self-serving, and there aren't any witnesses. It has to come from someone else. And there is only one person who can clear you," Lethajoy said.

"Angela?"

"Angela."

"Shit." Neal wondered how it could get more compli-
cated. He tipped his head back, ceiling tile filling his vision.
"Crazy, but with Hoopingartner holding the gun on me I
flashed on Kimo, the kid in the wheelchair in Hawaii." He
looked over at Yvonne, sitting next to him on the couch.
"Before then, I'd never seen a wheelchair. I mean that I saw
them but they didn't register, made no impression. Like no
one was sitting in them." Neal closed his eyes. "Then I pictured myself in one, bullet to the spine. Sounds strange to
say now, but I guess I'm lucky."

UNDER THE CIRCUMSTANCES, the Visiting Officers' Quarters manager allowed Yvonne to stay in Neal's reassigned
suite, a privilege usually denied wives of visiting officers
(though not necessarily to other temporary female guests).
His previous room was undergoing repair: new carpet and
couch, patching and painting the walls. The cops had batted .500, hitting Hoopingartner with half of the dozen
rounds they expended. The rest of the slugs tore up the real
estate while missing Neal.

Yvonne rinsed the carafe from the coffee maker and dried
it with one of the new dish towels she had picked up at the
Navy Exchange. She returned the carafe to the warming
plate. "I was thinking about all the lewd things we could do
here. Sort of feels illicit and sexy doing it in a government
building. It feels remote and slightly foreign, like the B&B
in Lahaina, minus the ambiance."

Neal chuckled at the comparison. "We'd have to figure
out some new positions you can do one-handed. Hoopingartner shot off one of my love handles."

"One way to take off a pound or two." She smiled and sat
next to him on the couch, one arm across his chest. "We'll

manage," she said and kissed him fully on the lips. "Tie one arm to the bedstead."

"I love you, Yvonne, but bondage will have to wait. Might rip my stitches."

"Oh, I know. It's just fun to think about it. I was going nuts at home, alone. Imagining things."

"I guess we could both use a little fun for a change." He gazed into her eyes and watched her smile fade, a look of curiosity rising as his silence lengthened, his expression turned serious. How could he say this, something that hadn't left his mind for days? "I've been thinking about changing my plea. I probably should have done it before now."

"Why? Why would you do that?" Yvonne's question came straight, emotion suppressed—not a *why, goddamnit!* but the kind of question a clerk might ask for the sake of information only, filling out a form. Perhaps nothing could surprise her anymore.

"There are a lot of reasons, but the main one is that a not-guilty plea is a lie."

"What does Lethajoy say?"

"She said that I'd sleep better—although maybe in jail. I wanted to discuss it with you first because you would have to live with the consequences, too."

Yvonne stood, walking a few paces to the center of the room. Turning toward him she said, "You're saying you want to just give up, let 'em throw you in prison?" She spread her hands wide. "Didn't you say this was a show trial to make up for all the ones who got off lightly?"

"That's the way it looks, but maybe they'll go easier if I don't make them work for a conviction. I'd have to gamble it'll keep me out of prison. Maybe they'll be satisfied with the humiliation. I could still lose the retirement pay and my clearances, maybe pay a fine. I'll still have to make a settlement with Defense Dynamics . . . but at least I'd be able to work somewhere . . . this wouldn't all fall on your—"

"That bitch!" Yvonne suddenly burst out. "Why'd she have to do this—ruin you to sell her stinking book, then testify against you and go on her way!" Yvonne balled her fists, arms stiff at her sides. "All those years that we put off having a family because it was the best thing for the navy and for your career. Now, the only chance we'll ever have is being snatched away." Angry tears welled in her eyes.

Neal left the couch, crossing to his wife, and put his arm around her shoulder, drawing her to him. "I'd give anything to change all this, Yvonne. I can't stand the thought of hurting you because I love you more than anything. I'd understand if you wanted to leave—not much future. . . ."

She drew back, the movement quick, wiping her eyes. "No. I've done that before. The separations, filing for divorce, all that. I'm never leaving you again so just shut up about that."

"One other thing you need to know: it's a matter of honor too," said Neal. "I wasn't going to testify because I would have had to lie. I can't lie about this or remain silent anymore."

She regarded him, then stepped back. "If that's what you have to do, there's something I have to know, Neal. Was Angela the only one or did you act like a sailor on cruise?"

He had been expecting this for years, afraid that a denial might not be believed. Now, on the eve of a confession of his infidelity in court, he could give her the truth she deserved. He took her hands in his. "Never."

"FORGET IT, NEAL. I understand what you want to do and the reasons, but I'm advising against it," Lethajoy said. Yvonne sat next to her husband in the VOQ suite.

"Under normal circumstances I wouldn't try to discourage you, but remember that there are charges against you for both adultery and conduct unbecoming. I can appreciate your devotion to honor, but this court is not a place where honor seems to matter that much, officially. Look at the judge's rulings so far, then argue honor. The thought of throwing this to the mercy of the court gives me shivers. We need to get this into the hands of the jury. They are officers like you and I trust them to be as honorable as we're likely to find. And like it or not, they are the only panel you're going to get."

After Lethajoy had gone, Neal and Yvonne ordered Chinese and opened a bottle of Merlot. In an odd way, Neal liked their impromptu, simple living arrangement, at least for the time being; it was much like when they had first married. What they did not have in material possessions lent greater fullness to their time together. Meals from white paper boxes were leisurely. No office work or cooking. In the morning, boiling water and instant grits—a breakfast habit Neal had picked up in Pensacola during Officer Candidate School.

And talk. Time to talk as they had at the beginning, before they married, when neither was fully sure of themselves or the other. Yvonne rested her head on the couch arm while Neal gently rubbed her feet and stroked her legs. He concentrated on her right foot, gently massaging, feeling the pair of small bony bumps that had developed after her teenage ballet accident. Neal thought about the way she moved now, with a gracefulness that belied her old injury. Only when she tired did her limp become apparent. The sensation he caused brought small satisfied moans. She began speaking softly, eyes closed, arms sprawled. "That's why I wanted a separation when you were on *Constellation*. We weren't getting any closer to having a child, and I was getting frustrated. Not that splitting up would have helped that situation. Adding it all up, I just found myself so unsatisfied, I'd sit at the kitchen table when you were at sea and just cry sometimes."

He lifted her foot and kissed her toes.

She drew her foot back a few inches and refocused her gaze on him. "You don't know where that's been."

He kissed it again. "I just know that it's here and I love it."

"Soooo romantic. Probably get hepatitis C, lockjaw, athlete's mouth, who knows," she said, giggling.

⬥★▐▐▐ CHAPTER THIRTEEN

Neal and Yvonne were waiting in the defense room when Lethajoy arrived at the legal center. Neal immediately stood when the lawyer entered. "I want to testify," he said quickly.

Lethajoy stopped, staring at him a moment before placing her briefcase on the table. "That isn't wise, Neal. I advise against it. Why should we let Merlin cross-examine?"

"I've got to do it," he said, reaching to take Yvonne's hand.

"What'll you say?" Lethajoy's face revealed both concern and recognition that she could not change his mind.

"I don't know," Neal said.

LETHAJOY SCANNED THE COURTROOM, the image of a grade-school teacher ensuring all were paying proper attention. It had been ten days of adjournment. Neal turned his body slowly in his straight-backed chair, unable to twist without triggering a sharp pain in his side. He watched the way his attorney stood, solid, like she could stop a train using intimidation and force of will. His admiration for

Lethajoy, as a person as well as a lawyer, had continued to build; although it had made him slightly uncomfortable at first, he was glad that she had taken him to the restaurant to meet Susan Lamply. And he realized it was not strictly in her job description to sit by his hospital bed.

Lethajoy had petitioned Judge Pickens to have the court reporter read aloud the prosecution's examination of Angela Vance, a request so basic to justice following the ten-day recess that for Sandra Pickens to refuse would have removed any lingering doubt that she had predetermined the outcome of this court-martial. This acquiescence came after her denials of defense motions for dismissal or a mistrial. Dismissal at this point would fail to serve the trial's purpose. Beginning again with a new panel was out of the question. The judge reasoned aloud that this case had already consumed too much time with Neal's absence.

The courtroom held all who had been present before the forced recess, minus Barney Pilcher, plus one. Yvonne, dressed today in a maroon skirt and jacket, sat back of the rail, behind the defense table. Angela Vance, occupying the witness box, captured in Yvonne's unblinking stare, averted her own eyes. She had been subdued since she had seen Neal and Yvonne walk into the legal center together.

Lethajoy came to her feet. "Ms. Vance, you've been getting a lot of attention because of your novel, *Navy Wench*. Part of that success, no doubt, is due to your implications on national television and in print media that one of the characters in the book is based on Commander Olen. Also that the protagonist, Gillian Lorenz, is your alter ego. Your book is the sole reason charges were initially brought against Neal Olen—"

"Is there a question in there somewhere, Ms. Beltower?" Pickens broke in.

"Yes, Your Honor. Ms. Vance, which of the other navy characters in your book are real people?"

"None of them are *real*, but they might be based on people I've known."

"When you say 'none are real,' how do you square that with your pointed insinuation that Allen Neil is Neal Olen? You make the connection that the accused is a navy hero."

"I never meant Neal. That was just a teaser in the TV interviews."

Neal leaned forward momentarily, a change of position that relieved some of the pressure on his bullet wound.

Lethajoy raised her hand to her head, as if to scratch it in confusion, a puzzled look on her face. Theatrics. "Then how do you explain that virtually anyone who had read your book and had seen last year's State of the Union address came to that conclusion?"

"Objection. The question calls for the witness to possess omniscience. Overly broad." Sutton spoke from his chair.

"Sustained. Panel, disregard."

Lethajoy continued without varying her tone, but Neal could detect a tightening of her shoulders. "Isn't it true, Ms. Vance, that you would say anything that would sell books?"

"Not *anything*. I just plant a seed, tickle the public's imagination and stand back. There are limits, though."

Lethajoy stepped forward, speaking faster, as though some salient point would otherwise slip away. "But those limits don't include Commander Olen?"

"How could I know the navy would take it so seriously? People have affairs every day. They don't go to jail for it, for God's sake. Gives 'unsafe sex' a whole other meaning." Angela smirked.

"Then I take it that you have no desire to be here, testifying."

"Who'd want to be here?"

A smile teased the lawyer's lips as she turned slightly toward the panel of officers in the jury box. "Of course, most of us would agree with you on that point. When Neal Olen visited you on the evening he was first attacked by your ex-husband, Kenneth Hoopingartner, what did you talk about?"

"As I said before, I told him I was sorry about the mess."

"And?"

"And . . . nothing."

Lethajoy bore in. "Isn't it true that you tried to convince Commander Olen to confess to the charges?"

"No."

"Isn't it true that you offered him a bribe to confess so your subpoena would be dropped, so you wouldn't have to testify?"

"No!"

"And isn't it true that when Commander Olen turned you down flat, you warned him that Kenneth Hoopingartner could be dangerous and he was very angry about having to testify? That he might do something violent?"

"You're making this up. It's bullshit."

Judge Pickens cut in, barely audible under the raised voices of Lethajoy and Angela. "Witness will refrain from obscenities."

Angela turned her head toward the judge with a blank *what-the-fuck?* expression most often encountered on a defiant teenager's face. The movement, the set of her face, carried a clear implication of disdain for the judge and everything else about the proceedings, encouraging Lethajoy to bear down on her, push a little harder.

"And isn't it true that your ex-husband feared that further investigation of Neal Olen would eventually lead the authorities to him, that Kenneth Hoopingartner would be revealed for having given you top secret information?"

"More bullshit."

"I warned you," Pickens barked, tapping the gavel.

Lethajoy stalked the few steps to the defense table. Picking up a copy of *Navy Wench*, she opened it as she crossed back to Angela and glanced at the judge. "I've marked a passage in your book, near the end. Please read it aloud."

Angela's gaze shifted from Lethajoy's face to the offered book and back. Slowly she took it and scanned the underlined text.

> *Gillian pointedly yawned. Sure, it was mildly interesting that the Keyhole-11 spy satellite gave the first evidence that the Iraqi Army was advancing on Kuwait, but she couldn't have cared less about Sam's clearances, his efforts to impress her—or about Sam. He was turning out to be another navy doofus who thought the secrets he picked up aboard ship would be enough to unlock her secrets, hoist her skirt.*

Angela snapped the book shut and laid it on the rail.

"Objection," Merlin Sutton blurted. "Ms. Vance is not on trial, nor is her late ex-husband. Irrelevant and possibly a compromise of classified material."

"What are you trying to prove here?" Judge Pickens leaned across the bench, gavel at the ready, waving threateningly in her hand. "Approach."

Sutton came from behind his table. Lethajoy stepped to the bench, facing Pickens straight on. "Judge, this passage is part of the novel the prosecution placed into evidence. And during the Article 32 hearing in this case, Agent Godat revealed an investigation of Commander Olen into a possible compromise of classified material related to this book, Your Honor."

"That has no relevance in this court-martial. There are no charges," Sutton broke in before Pickens could respond. She shot him a withering glare as Lethajoy continued.

"Your Honor, the relevance here is to additional charges that could very well be brought against my client at any moment, prolonging his ordeal. I beg that you allow this line of questioning so that there will be a record of how Angela Vance came to know about this material that subsequently showed up in her book, which *is* relevant."

"Judge, I object," Sutton said. "Your Honor, this is so far afield as to be ridiculous."

Lethajoy faced Pickens. "Your Honor, I submit that it's true that this is highly irregular. I also point out that Commander Olen has been viciously attacked twice, nearly losing his life, also irregular. That he—a decorated navy intelligence officer—is under apparent suspicion of having given away government secrets." She modulated her voice, slowing. "Your Honor, we can learn the truth of it here in a few minutes. There may never be another, or better, opportunity. And no matter what the verdict here, Commander Olen should not have to bear the false stain of flouting his oath to protect national secrets."

Pickens exhaled slowly, considering, glancing at the jury stiffly upright in their chairs. "As reluctant as I am, I nevertheless feel compelled to allow it. Make it short." Neal leaned forward, intent. Finally, a break from the judge, an opportunity to establish his innocence, at least on this point.

"I remind you that you're under oath, Ms. Vance." Lethajoy returned to her earlier position in front of the witness box. "Did Kenneth Hoopingartner ever mention Keyhole or any other military satellites to you?"

After a pause Angela began. "I guess it doesn't matter now. Yes, he told me, but I never paid that much attention at the time. He was always spouting off about secret this and secret that, like he was some kind of James Bond. But he just worked in a photo lab on the ship."

"When did he talk about Keyhole?" Lethajoy said, raising her prominent eyebrows.

"Well, we were married and Ken had just been assigned to the *Constellation*, so it must have been '92 or '93."

"How did you come to mention the Keyhole-11 satellite in *Navy Wench*?"

Angela smiled, warming to the subject. "I needed something for a character, Sam, the chief petty officer, to brag about. I remembered Ken had said something about the satellites so I checked the Internet and there it was."

Lethajoy said, "And you first met Commander Olen in late 1995, before you wrote *Navy Wench*. Did commander Olen ever mention Keyhole or other classified material to you?"

"No."

"So the mysterious 'source' of information that you alluded to on television was your ex-husband and *not* Commander Olen?"

"Yes," Angela said.

"Isn't it true that you wanted to avoid testifying because if you tell the truth here, then you cannot hide behind the disclaimer in the front of *Navy Wench* that any resemblance to real people is coincidental—because you don't want to be sued, or worse, by people whose lives you portray? You rely on that disclaimer for plausible deniability. Isn't that right?"

"It *is* fiction," Angela tossed off.

"On the other hand, you make no secret that it isn't *very* fiction—only *a little* fiction—because that helps sell books, while destroying, or certainly complicating, other people's lives. This is just part of your book-marketing plan. Certainly, this court-martial will stir up interest, but so would a confession to the charges by Commander Olen, with a lot less inconvenience for you. So you wanted the publicity, but you needed Commander Olen to confess so neither you nor Ken would have to face him in court. Isn't that right?"

Seconds passed. Pickens spoke. "Witness will please answer the question."

"You don't understand," Angela protested, visibly flustered.

"Oh, but I do understand, Ms. Vance. Bribery and threats did not work on Commander Olen, so from your window you signaled Kenneth Hoopingartner, who was waiting outside, to do the job with a baseball bat. Isn't *that* right?"

"No. Kenneth had been threatening *me*, watching *my* house. That must have been the reason he was out there and just took the opportunity. I had tried to get a restraining order against him."

"Perhaps if Kenneth Hoopingartner had not been killed by police during his *second* attack on Commander Olen, we could ask him," said Lethajoy. "He might have had a better memory than your own. But now there is no one else who can refute your story. Good for book sales, right? Makes you way more interesting to have a stalker ex-husband who is eventually killed in the act of attacking Commander Olen. Wouldn't Dagmar love to interview you on television about that?"

A glimmer of something that looked like fear or surprise crossed Angela's face before her expression returned to steel. "Go ahead and dig the motherfucker up. Ask him."

"I wish we could, Ms. Vance, but since we cannot, I guess we'll have to rely on the legacy you left for him in *Navy Wench*. I'm through with this witness, Your Honor."

Sutton got to his feet, leading Angela through a recap of her earlier testimony, hammering on her admission of having had sex with Neal.

When he'd finished, Judge Pickens, who had begun to look bored with the repetition, spoke up. "If you have no further witnesses, Commander Sutton, Ms. Beltower may present her case. Witness is excused. Counsel, do you have any witnesses?"

"Yes, Your Honor. Call Commander Neal Edward Olen," Lethajoy said.

Neal felt a stab of regret hearing his name, recognizing that the time had come to test his honor, to say his piece under Lethajoy's guiding questions, then submit to Merlin Sutton's scrutiny. Can't have one without the other, Lethajoy had told him while trying to prepare him to face cross-examination.

Angela Vance, released from the witness box, paused near the defense table. "Sorry, Neal," she said simply and walked to the door.

Neal felt a hand on his shoulder. Lethajoy. Rising from the chair pulled at his stitched wound. The pain, no longer searing, was still unmistakably there. He had abandoned the pain pills, slipping the prescription vial into Yvonne's purse for later. He would endure the discomfort for a clear mind on the stand. He had begun walking haltingly since taking the bullet to avoid putting strain on his side. Now he stood straight, strode to the witness box and raised his right hand as high as he could as the bailiff approached.

He turned slightly in the witness chair and locked eyes with Yvonne. She returned a tiny smile and a nod. The courtroom receded into an envelope of white sound, everything far away, as he gazed into her eyes. He flashed on the Kaiwi Channel, Kimo's frightened face in the choppy sea, not understanding anything but terror. Neal trying to comfort the helpless child with his tuneless rendition of "Barnacle Bill the Sailor." Then the face became his own at eleven years, but the only sound was lapping of the surrounding sea. No one was singing.

"Do you swear or affirm that the evidence you shall give in this case now in hearing shall be the truth, the whole truth, and nothing but the truth?"

"I do."

"Commander Olen," Lethajoy began, "you have heard the testimony against you. What can you add that will assist the panel in their deliberations?"

Neal drew a breath, heart pounding, and began, "I do not refute the testimony given here."

A rustle of movement filled the room. Yvonne dipped her head, put her hand to her forehead, but composed herself again quickly. Sutton broke a smile and laid his pen and yellow pad on the table before him, leaning back. His expression said *victory*.

Neal went on, "Certain details are, I believe, incorrect, but I will not waste the court's time with inconsequential matters. I want the president and members of the panel to know that I deeply regret my actions—when I put my marriage vows aside and gave in to impulse. I regret everything that has accrued from my actions, the shame I brought to my wife," he gazed pointedly at Yvonne across the room, "and my tarnished honor as a naval officer. Most especially, I am sorry that Petty Officer Kenneth Hoopingartner died, in part, as an outgrowth of my infidelity. Perhaps it's a remote connection but a connection, still." He drew a breath before going on.

"What I can say in my defense is that at no time were naval operations or the functioning or morale of my ship ever compromised by what I did. I am grateful that my wife has forgiven me, though it will be many years before I can forgive myself—if ever."

Lethajoy allowed Neal's words to end and for silence to return and endure a full ten seconds before speaking. "Commander Olen, you are making an admission that you engaged in an adulterous affair but that it had no impact on your effectiveness as an officer . . . ?"

"That is right."

". . . or the effectiveness of your subordinates or others in the navy while you were assigned to USS *Constellation* or during later active duty assignments?"

"That is correct."

"Are you aware that the penalty for adultery under the UCMJ can include loss of your retirement benefits and up to a year in prison?"

"It has never left my mind."

"Why, then, do you admit to the affair with Angela Vance?"

"Because that is the truth," Neal said, "because it is the only way to begin redeeming my honor."

"Do you believe that what you did ought not be a military crime?" Lethajoy enunciated carefully.

"It was a crime at the time I accepted my commission over twenty years ago and has been since. What I think now cannot matter."

"Do you have anything else to say, Commander—"

"The witness will not speak!" The judge cut in with a rap of the gavel. Her voice rose. "Counsel, you'll save mitigating testimony for presentencing. I don't want to hear it now."

"But, Your Honor—"

Judge Sandra Pickens rose off her chair and leaned forward, pointing at Lethajoy with the gavel. "You heard me. Now refrain from this line or face contempt."

"Yes, Your Honor." Lethajoy turned to Neal, her eyes like a leprechaun's. "Thank you for your testimony and honesty, Commander. No further questions."

"Trial counsel, cross-examination?"

"Yes, ma'am." Sutton presented a triumphant face to the panel, then turned to Neal. "Commander, you admit to adultery but not to conduct unbecoming?"

"Yes," Neal said, his voice strengthening.

"I'm curious as to why you don't admit to both. Adultery certainly *sounds* to me, and I would expect to the panel—"

"Objection. This is examination, not argument," said Lethajoy.

Pickens drew a breath, reluctant. "Save your suspicions about the panel's beliefs for arguments, Commander Sutton. Counsel are warned not to get ahead of the bench."

"Let me rephrase. Isn't it true that adultery is, on its face, most clearly conduct unbecoming an officer and gentleman?"

"I am not an expert on the UCMJ so I can't say for sure." Neal's voice remained flat, his response factual.

"Surely you have read the elements. Surely your actions qualify."

"Objection. Trial counsel should make his own case and not rely on the accused to do it for him." Lethajoy spoke from the table.

"Witness will answer."

Neal thought a moment, framing his response. "I have read the elements but cannot see how I meet them all. At no time was morale affected."

"Why don't you just admit to the charge of conduct unbecoming an officer and gentleman—as long as you're freely admitting to adultery? We can get this over with right now, or are you trying to play games with this court?"

"Objection, Your Honor. This isn't a two-for-one sale," said Lethajoy, a smile flickering over her face.

"Witness will answer."

"None of this feels like a game to me, Commander Sutton. As I understand my right against self-incrimination, I'm not obligated to admit anything or even to testify."

"What does your attorney say about your independent analysis of the charges—"

"Objection! Attorney-client privilege." Lethajoy was on her feet.

Sutton looked confused for a moment. "I withdraw the question and apologize to the court."

Judge Pickens pulled an exasperated look. "Wherever you're going with this, please get on with it—you've already been presented with an admission."

Sutton looked blankly at Judge Pickens. "Ah . . . no further questions, Your Honor."

"I don't suppose you want to redirect?" Pickens said, staring at Lethajoy.

"No, Your Honor," Lethajoy responded.

"Commander Olen, you may step down. We will adjourn for lunch. Reconvene at thirteen thirty."

"FEEL BETTER?" LETHAJOY looked across the top of a hamburger bun at Neal.

"A little, but it seems like I just stepped into an alligator's soup bowl."

"Honor is a demanding bitch, isn't she?" Lethajoy bit into her sandwich as if she wished it were Judge Sandra Pickens's arm.

Yvonne curled a hand around Neal's arm. "I'm proud of him. Scared, embarrassed, but proud. My stomach's still all funny from listening to the testimony."

Neal gently squeezed Yvonne's knee. Looking across the table he said to his lawyer, "So now what?" Neal flashed on the correctional custody unit he had visited, the cages, the silence, the marine guards. He pushed his sandwich away and took a sip of water.

The attorney finished chewing. "First there'll be arguments where I try to get everyone to forget what you said and Sutton tries to get them to remember that a confession to adultery is as good as a confession to the conduct unbecoming charge. But I suspect that the jury will take your career record into account when we get into sentencing." Lethajoy sipped her drink and leaned forward on her elbows. "They're officers, like you, but they are also men. You can bet that not one of them hasn't been at least tempted by an 'Angela.'"

While Neal considered this, Yvonne spoke. "Everyone gets tempted. Human nature's hard to overcome."

"That's the whole point of military discipline, to be better than human nature makes us," Lethajoy said. "If you give in to human nature, you save your ass by running for cover. But that's just when the navy expects you to stand up and fight." Lethajoy leaned back. "And where are you going to run to when your ship's on fire, when cruise missiles are incoming?"

"Part of it's training," Neal offered for Yvonne's benefit. "Knowing how to fight, how to save your ship, becomes a programmed response. The rest's military culture. Cowardice and dishonor have no part."

"So, what you're saying is that Neal is being court-martialed for being too much like a civilian," said Yvonne.

Lethajoy snorted a laugh. "Mostly for getting caught." The lawyer turned to Yvonne, warming to her favorite subject. "The Uniform Code of Military Justice is a truly wondrous document that can be made to cover whatever an imaginative prosecutor might want. Let's stick to sex, which seems to be a military favorite. Say that a married sailor goes into town intent on getting a little nooky since he's in a faraway place. But he's a sexual klutz and doesn't score. He's still guilty of Article 80, 'attempts' at adultery—getting screwed for not getting screwed."

"Got one against lusting in your heart?" Yvonne asked, a rueful smile on her lips, clearly willing to leave Neal's case aside for the moment.

"Something almost as good." Lethajoy said. "This same married sailor suggests to his married buddy they both go out on liberty and pick up a couple of hookers. Sailor A is guilty of Article 134, soliciting another to commit an offense, *and* adultery *or* attempts, maybe a pandering and prostitution charge, too. Sailor B will probably get nailed with a charge of adultery or attempts. If it happens to be a couple of officers, married or not, it's also conduct unbecoming."

"Yeah, wondrous," Neal said. "Not really what I want to hear at the moment."

Lethajoy glanced at Neal, then turned back to Yvonne. "The point is, military law is highly flexible. My all-time favorite is 'abusing a public animal,' which includes wild animals in a national park."

MERLIN SUTTON STOOD BEFORE the panel of five officers, hands in the air before him, palms up, as though offering them a serving of logic. "Gentlemen, Commander Neal Edward Olen has openly admitted to this court that he did, indeed, commit the specified acts of adultery, making your task of finding him guilty very easy." Sutton paced in front of the rail, speaking slowly. Lethajoy would get a single chance to make a closing argument, then he would go a second time in rebuttal.

"On the basis of that admission, you can find the accused guilty as well of conduct unbecoming an officer and gentleman—the second charge. You must ask yourselves: Under the circumstances, did Commander Olen's admitted adultery constitute conduct unbecoming an officer and gentleman, and was the ship's crew affected? The finding of only one of these is necessary. Ask, as an officer yourself, if you want to be associated in public and military thought with an adulterer.

"In the navy—in *our* navy—in over two centuries of service in arms to our country, we have held ourselves to significantly higher standards of conduct than the citizens we are sworn to protect. Is it fair? Fairness is, and should be, a poor second to moral excellence.

"A two-thirds majority is enough for conviction." Merlin Sutton swept his gaze over the five-officer panel, offering them a tight-lipped smile. "Gentlemen, I know you will do the right thing." Merlin walked to his chair and sat, straightening his notes, mouth pursed, smug.

"Gentlemen." Lethajoy approached the panel. "You alone control the outcome of this court-martial. You have complete freedom to make *whatever* choice you feel is just, not only what is in the statutes. Not me, not the prosecution, not even the judge can make up your minds once you enter the deliberation room—"

"Stop right there," Judge Pickens broke in. "I sense where you are going with this line of argument and I won't allow it. You risk contempt, Ms. Beltower."

"I'm sorry, Your Honor, but I'm not sure I understand what you mean," Lethajoy responded.

"Counsel, approach," Pickens said.

Sutton came forward, joining Lethajoy at the bench. Neal strained to hear the whispered discussion without success. He cleared his throat, drawing Lethajoy's attention. Sutton returned to his table wearing a slight smile.

"Your Honor, if I may consult with my client?" Lethajoy did not wait for an answer but returned to the defense table.

"What are you doing?" Neal asked in an urgent whisper, angry that Lethajoy was sparring with the judge.

Lethajoy leaned close. "I'm telling the jury to ignore your guilty plea, to act as the court's conscience. If they find you not guilty, the judge can't direct a guilty verdict, the prosecution can't appeal, and you can't be court-martialed twice. It'll be over with, which is why Sandra Pickens and every other judge hates it."

"Isn't it a gamble?" Neal said, his anger abating.

"It's all that's left, Neal. Time to punt."

Lethajoy turned back to the judge and, with a chastened expression, continued her argument. "The penalty for adultery, if you choose to bring in a conviction, may be as severe as a loss of all pay and allowances and a year in prison. A conviction here, even if you decide on awarding no punishment, will strip Commander Olen of his top secret clearance and any chance to continue in his chosen second career. So, gentlemen, it is indeed a big hammer that you wield.

"You might be thinking that Neal Olen should have thought of the possible consequences before committing an act that could turn out to be a UCMJ offense. The offense, however, pales when compared to the punishment and the collateral damage to Commander Olen's life.

"Then you must ask yourself whether this smacks of vengeance rather than justice." Lethajoy locked each juror in a penetrating gaze, one after the other.

"*If only* Commander Olen had given in to Angela Vance's attempts at bribery, we wouldn't be spending our time searching for the truth. He would have pled guilty at the outset.

"*If only* Commander Olen had caved in to Angela Vance's threats, Petty Officer Kenneth Hoopingartner would probably be alive today. Do we convict him for that, for wanting his day in court?

"*If only* Neal and Yvonne Olen had not separated in November 1995 and had not been on the cusp of a divorce. . . .

"But we cannot change history, we can only deal with it intelligently and compassionately. The military system uses the prohibition against adultery, like that against fraternization, as a tool to maintain good order and discipline. In Commander Olen's case, good order and discipline were *never* threatened. When you retire for deliberation, ask yourself whether Commander Neal Edward Olen ought to be convicted of anything."

Gavel! "Panel shall disregard that last statement. Ms. Beltower, you are in contempt. I warned you about straying to that line of argument at the outset."

"My apologies, Your Honor, but there is no prohibition in the *Manual for Courts-Martial* against such a defense argument."

"Nevertheless. Finish your argument but recognize that I view it with hostility. A sense of trepidation would serve you well. I'll deal with your contempt penalty later."

"Thank you, Your Honor, I'm through."

Judge Pickens wasted no time, rising as she spoke. "We will reconvene here tomorrow morning at 0900. Then I will instruct the panel. Perhaps we can conclude the penalty phase tomorrow as well. Adjourned."

"WHAT DOES THE CONTEMPT charge mean?" Neal asked Lethajoy as they walked down the corridor outside the courtroom.

"First, it means that I'm through, but I was through anyway. I was letting the jury know the breadth of its autonomy. Judges hate that, which is why it also means thirty days or a hundred bucks or both. Think I'd rather have the fine. The hundred bucks I can put on your bill, but I'd have to do jail myself."

"Is there a chance she'll give you jail time?" Yvonne looked concerned.

"I don't think she can make it stick. Some judges like to throw around the threat like she's been doing. It makes 'em sound ballsy and in control. She just didn't like my argument. Sandra knew exactly where I was going, though it is a seldom-trod, seldom-successful path. I don't think what I did rises anywhere close to the level of actual contempt. That takes a 'menacing word, sign, or gesture or a disturbance by any riot or disorder,' if I remember Article 48 correctly. No, she just didn't want the jury members to remember the extent of their own power."

"Sounded pretty riled up to me," Neal said. His side was starting to throb. "Let me have those pain pills, Yvonne. I've got no need for a clear head now, would rather not have one."

Yvonne removed the cap from the vial for Neal, who had been discovering how hard it was to operate with one hand splinted.

Lethajoy left Neal and Yvonne in the passageway, returning from the judge's chambers after a few minutes. "She just took the hundred bucks because she thought that I wouldn't protest. And I won't. Not yet. I'll save it for later. The old bat's way off base. Still, I don't need a contempt charge. Wouldn't look good with the state bar or in the yellow pages," Lethajoy said wryly. Then the lawyer insisted Neal and Yvonne come to her apartment for dinner. "Can't refuse. I already called ahead and soup's on."

CHAPTER FOURTEEN

W hen the three arrived at the Hillcrest townhouse, the aroma of sautéing garlic filled the air. "Susan," Lethajoy called out, slipping off her coat. "Our guests are here." Susan emerged from the kitchen in an ankle-length bamboo-print skirt and a black shell top. She gave Lethajoy a quick kiss on her lips, then extended a hand. "Yvonne, this is Susan Lamply. Susan, you know Neal."

"Welcome." Susan spoke softly, a seductive tone of voice.

"Smells good in here," said Yvonne.

"Susan's the cook in this bunch," Lethajoy commented to Yvonne. "When she's not feeding me here she's sous-chef at À la Bonne Heure."

"I've got to get back to the kitchen." Susan stepped back a pace.

"May I come with you?" Yvonne asked quickly. "Watch a real chef in action?"

"Great," Susan said and the two women disappeared around a corner.

Neal glanced around the large, modern living room. It overlooked Lindbergh Field airport in the distance. In a glass-front curio cabinet was a collection of scrimshaw and ivory carvings. The central piece, nearly a foot long, depicted a polar bear and walrus carved in high relief along the length of a walrus tusk–shaped base. Around it were arranged other scrimshaw items—ivory pistol grips, a woman's comb and brush, a shoe horn—that revealed their design in etched lines filled with India ink.

Neal moved closer to the glass balcony door. The airport was far enough away that the commercial jets' noise dissipated to a whisper before reaching the hillside apartment, but it was close enough to provide a spectacular sunset and evening view. Neal watched the bay-reflected light from Coronado and the shadow cast against the sky by the thousand-foot navy aircraft carrier tied at the North Island pier. Like all the carriers, it displayed a huge painted number below the navigation bridge. Outlined with lights, the twenty-foot-high "64" was the USS *Constellation*. The *Connie* was almost forty years old and approaching retirement. Neal wondered if he could wrangle a final tour of the carrier. He had to admit to himself that in spite of the court-martial he still felt pride in his own service and in the navy. He could almost convince himself what was happening to him was an anomaly, that the real navy was directly in front of him in floating gray steel.

"Martini?" Lethajoy had moved in quietly behind him.

"Sure. I was admiring your scrimshaw."

"It was my father's. Left it to me when he died. The bear and walrus piece was his favorite, but he also had an ivory toilet seat he liked to show people. That's the one I keep hidden," she said with a laugh. Lethajoy crossed to the breakfast bar where a variety of bottles and glasses had been set out. She mixed drinks for them all and joined Neal near the gas log fireplace. Motioning to a black leather couch for him to sit, she said, "He was a chief boatswain's mate."

"Daddy's girl," Neal said, recalling that she had told him that's why she joined the navy. "Too bad it didn't work out for you. Navy's always crying for good, competent people."

She raised her glass and took the first sip of her bourbon. "To the navy. Cheers."

"Thanks for having us over," Neal said. "The VOQ and takeout food's a bit more tolerable now that Yvonne's here, but it still gets a little tiresome. Though I expect it will beat the hell out of military prison rations."

Lethajoy drew a serious face. "I'd like to tell you not to worry about prison, Neal, but realistically I can't do that. I just don't know how this will go—too much extra pressure bearing on the case. I've been trying to read the panel from the start, but they're pretty stoic. They don't show much emotion other than a chuckle or two in the right places. Though they sure paid attention to Angela. Who wouldn't?" She adjusted her position, turning to face him directly. "Trouble with military juries is that they give nothing away. Captain Posey, the president, is the key. They're all supposed to be independent thinkers in the deliberation room, but they're so used to doing what the senior man wants during the rest of their professional lives that most of them will probably fall in behind him. Trouble is, he isn't telegraphing a thing."

Neal considered her words and suddenly wanted to hear nothing more about the court-martial. Enough. He had always been reluctant to ask personal questions of friends, didn't want them to feel like he was prying, a reaction to his U.S. overseas consulate assignments where inconspicuous prying was part of the job. But he had begun to feel close to Lethajoy, developed a trust. Maybe it was a variety of the camaraderie soldiers feel when counting on each other for survival.

"How did you and Susan meet?" He admitted to himself that he knew nothing about gays, hadn't cared before now. "I have to confess to some curiosity and some naiveté. Is it like wearing a flower over your left ear as a signal?"

Lethajoy laughed. "I suppose you could say there is a particular language, but it's not like Esperanto, nothing agreed upon. It is something you develop around straight people. Never identify gender or names, you know, like 'we went to a movie' or 'my friend and I took a drive.'"

"That must get tedious, watching your words like that all the time," Neal said, sipping his drink, feeling the gin magnify the effect of the pain pills, getting comfortable before the fireplace.

"Yeah, plus anyone listening closely could figure it out pretty quickly. On the other hand, it's a good way to identify another queer. It's how I met Susan. We were both in a pottery class. One of those college extension things, supposed to be good for the inner self. We were both trying to relax, get away from the job. She was doing beautiful work with the clay. Me, I was turning it back into mud. Got to talking and figured it out pretty quickly. It just grew from there. I was still in the navy then, but not for long."

"The forced resignation."

"Yeah. One of those shitty coincidences that happens no matter how careful you try to be. Susan and I took a weekend trip to Santa Ynez Valley. Stayed in a bed-and-breakfast at a little out-of-the-way winery. Sandra Pickens had the room next door. Can you believe it?" Lethajoy's face hardened.

"How did she conclude you were gay? Women stay together all the time on vacation trips."

Lethajoy laughed through her nose and threw her head back. "That's where we got too confident that we had escaped the tight-assed navy. Sandra saw us in the hallway, kissing. Not sisterly kissing either. It was dumb, but by then we were feeling free and horny." A tiny smile crossed her lips as she paused, remembering. "I didn't know we'd been seen until Captain Jules Watembach called me into his office the next Monday and offered me an ultimatum. I could either resign or be tossed out. Of course that wasn't the end of it. He made sure that everyone knew."

Neal took it in. "A real gentleman, huh?"

"That was almost five years ago. He actually did me a favor. Once you're outed it's an incredible relief. Now I don't give a flying fuck who sees me with Susan. I can be honest with my clients, my friends . . . and with myself." Lethajoy drained the bourbon glass and stood. "I'll check on dinner."

Neal watched her cross the room and could hear Yvonne and Susan laughing in the kitchen. Lethajoy's story was oddly comforting. Somehow tomorrow's potential guilty verdict did not seem so dire as it had a few hours ago.

"LETHAJOY IS A BRILLIANT lawyer, but I've got to handle the finances," Susan revealed over dinner. "When she heard about *E. coli*, she thought it was an Internet start-up and wanted to invest."

That had been the tenor of conversation throughout the exquisite meal that had included scampi and new potatoes with rosemary. Dinner was nearing its finish and two bottles of sauvignon blanc had been drained. Laughter erupted among the four with less and less provocation.

Susan and Lethajoy stood at the door, comfortably together, each giving Yvonne a warm hug and momentarily squeezing Neal's hands.

"'Til morning then," Lethajoy said, looking Neal full in the face.

THEY LAY NAKED ON the double bed in the VOQ, having overcome, with imagination and passion, the limits of movement imposed by Neal's injuries. They had done their best to pleasure each other using hands and mouths and had done well, for it could be their last chance for a while. Now, as exhaustion had overtaken them, Yvonne adjusted her position next to her husband, lying on her side, face on his chest.

"I had a wonderful time at dinner. You?" Neal murmured.

"Mmmm," Yvonne said softly against his chest.

"In a funny way I'm not so scared anymore. Imagine the crap they both put up with just to live. Them against the world." He turned his head to the side and kissed her hair. "I never knew. My idea had always been women together in porno flicks, or those females-in-prison movies, all that. You notice how much they're like us, like an old married couple?

"Well, maybe not like me in that way," he paused, thinking. "My mistake was I didn't need anybody or anything, I thought. Just be the best intelligence officer I could and everything else would fall into place." He gazed at the ceiling, the institutional acoustic tiles with a wide water stain.

"Keep talking," Yvonne said sleepily.

"Almost losing you because of it." He sighed and drew her tighter to him.

CHAPTER FIFTEEN

Judge Pickens had instructed the panel immediately on opening the session. She then recessed the court for deliberations, retiring to chambers, leaving everyone else to kill time.

"Let's get out of here," Lethajoy said. "Keep your minds off it." She left her cell phone number at the legal center reception desk and drove Neal and Yvonne a few miles to a coffee shop in National City known for its fresh pies. Rain had begun early that morning and continued steadily under a lowering sky. Neal watched it out the plate glass window.

"Too bad they don't serve a brunch during the week," Lethajoy commented. "I always want to pig out waiting for a jury. Good thing I don't have a lot of trials. Like my mother used to say, I'd fall away to a ton." No one laughed. Neal allowed a slight elevation of one corner of his mouth. The laughter of the previous night had been good, but it did not last until morning. The lovemaking with Yvonne had also been good, their improvisations liberating and satisfying, but that hadn't lasted beyond the night either.

"Speaking of food, it was so sweet of you to invite us for dinner. We'd love to reciprocate. Maybe the next time you two are driving up the coast you could stop at our hou—" Yvonne stopped, apparently remembering that they might not have a house before long. An embarrassed look crossed her face.

Neal said nothing. His mind again raced over everything in his life that had led to this point—this turning point—and ended with him wondering at his personal history's significance. Then he attempted the converse view. Maybe it was time for a change, time to get away from the navy, from government contracting. Just forget the retirement angle; he was too young to call himself retired anyway. What better time to change careers, when the one you have has been snatched away.

A few sips of the coffee turned his stomach sour, and he declined the warm-up the waitress offered. Lethajoy, without embarrassment, ordered a second slice of lemon meringue and another latté and had just truncated the point of the pie with her fork when her cell phone sounded.

"Yes? OK. Ten minutes." She turned off the phone. "They're ready to announce." She took a quick bite of the pie and slid out of the booth. "That was fast."

Neal quickly pushed up from the booth, pulling his side, wincing. He slowed, asking himself, *Why so eager?*

JUDGE PICKENS CALLED THE court to order and nodded to the bailiff, who opened a side door to let the panel of officers in. They walked to the jury box and sat in their rank-alternate order. "Captain Posey, have the members reached findings?" asked the judge.

"Yes."

"Would the bailiff, without examining it, please bring me the findings," Pickens said.

Receiving it, the judge unfolded the sheet, reading carefully, silently; her eyes returning to the top, she read again. "It appears to be in proper form. Bailiff, please return this to the president." She released it reluctantly. "Commander Neal Edward Olen, would you and Ms. Beltower stand up and approach the president."

Neal and Lethajoy stood in front of the rail separating them from the panel of officers. Neal came to attention.

"Captain Posey, announce the findings, please." Pickens's voice came with a slight tremble.

The four remaining officers on the panel stood, flanking Posey, countenances blank, jaws firm, eyes on Neal.

The president stood and opened the paper. "On the specification of Conduct Unbecoming an Officer and Gentleman, this court-martial finds you not guilty."

Neal drew a quick breath at the unexpected verdict and focused on Captain Posey's command star in order to keep his own face neutral.

"On the specification of adultery, this court-martial finds you . . ." Posey raised his eyes to Neal, his own face stony. "Not guilty."

Neal felt an involuntary shudder and pressure behind his eyes, threatening tears of relief. Lethajoy hissed, "Yesss," restraining her volume with clenched teeth.

Not guilty? Neal could not understand. He had made an admission to the court, had given them their verdict. The shooting pain in his side reminded him he had been standing at attention, back stiffly arched, arms like rods to his side. He felt Lethajoy's hand on his back and relaxed a millimeter.

Posey spoke again. "This court-martial further finds that while Commander Olen's admitted conduct was reprehensible, it does not rise to a level justifying recall and punishment under the Uniform Code of Military Justice." Posey turned toward Judge Pickens. "This court-martial orders that barring any other clear and justifiable prohibition, Commander Olen's security clearances be reinstated immediately, Your Honor."

"The panel will please be seated. The accused, or rather, I should say, Commander Olen and Ms. Beltower, please be seated." As he crossed to the defense table, Neal exchanged a look with Yvonne, communicating in their own silent language. Neal and Lethajoy took their chairs in the stunned silence in the room.

Sutton was on his feet. "Your Honor, objection. This is unheard of. There was an admission—"

The gavel smacked the bench. "Commander Sutton, you know this outcome is undesirable in the extreme, but it is *not* unheard of. This court-martial is closed."

"But Your Honor—"

"Shut up, Merlin."

OUTSIDE THE COURTROOM, A gaggle of reporters roiled in the passageway, vying for position in the confines of the government building, allowed inside this time, no doubt, to be on hand instantly following the verdict. Yvonne stood close against Neal, protecting his wounded side from the shoving crowd.

"Why was Commander Olen acquitted? We were told he confessed," said a reporter in the front.

Lethajoy raised her palms, asking silence, a futile request as she shouted her answer over the babble. "It's clear from the verdict that the jury saw that the case against my client was elementally flawed and that the navy was conducting a witch-hunt. It's jury nullification. Remember this—you won't see it often in military cases."

"Commander Olen, how do you feel?"

Neal stared back at the questioner, a young, sport jacket–clad reporter he recognized from a local television station. "I'm happy the ordeal is over, and I owe my freedom to Ms. Beltower and the five officers on the panel who didn't like the show." What else could he possibly say? That he was still angry for having been dragged through a personal hell to be made an example of?

Lethajoy stepped a half pace forward. "Commander Olen is obviously pleased with the outcome. Now, if you'll excuse us." She led Neal and Yvonne along the packed hallway. A petty officer approached, wedging between bodies, and spoke briefly to Lethajoy, leaning close to her ear. She turned and said to Neal, "We have to pick up some paperwork inside, and I suspect there'll be some questions you'll have to answer."

They peeled away from the group of reporters with their microphones raised in the air like lances above a Roman legion. The hallway containing the admin office and the commanding officer's suite was markedly quieter than the press-packed passageway. Captain Watembach, the legal center commanding officer, stood outside his office talking animatedly with Merlin Sutton. Watembach waved Sutton away, then advanced toward them. "Please come in for a moment, Commander, Mrs. Olen, and, of course, the real hero of the day, Ms. Beltower." He effected a smile and shoved a large politician paw toward the three. They followed him into his office.

"This won't take long. They are preparing your release orders in the admin office." Watembach swung his arm, indicating a group of chairs for them to take, then rounded his desk. "First, let me congratulate you on your win. Lethajoy is a fine litigator, as we have all seen, as we've known around here for quite some time." Tossing off this comment as he would to a street beggar, Captain Watembach's insincerity was palpable.

Lethajoy, wearing her own amused face, spoke up. "Spare us the soft soap, Captain. It isn't going to change the fact that this case was bogus from the start. It was supposed to turn my client into a sacrificial lamb and make everyone forget about all the senior officers you let get away with far worse. You overplayed your hand."

"Sure, I understand that the perception is not very good among the civilian population. But the navy is doing its utmost to address that," Watembach said.

"I see," Lethajoy responded. "So Commander Olen was tried for bad public relations, not adultery. You might think about putting a brass plaque on the wall: 'On this site Captain Jules Watembach presided over the first total jury nullification in modern military history.'"

"Gloating does not become you, Lethajoy," Watembach said.

"I'll donate the first hundred bucks for the plaque," Lethajoy continued. "Once I get it back from Sandra Pickens for that bullshit contempt charge."

Captain Watembach glared at Lethajoy for an instant, then turned to Neal and Yvonne. "I'm sure you both want to put this all behind you." Yvonne nodded. Neal waited to hear the rest. "Take it from me: the best thing you can do for yourselves and for the navy is to say as little as possible to the press about this unfortunate chapter. You know how the press can be, distorting everything you say."

Neal stood. "Are you asking for my loyalty and discretion, Captain?"

"Of course, Commander, I see that you understand, a career officer such as yourself, there should be no question at all in the media about your fidelity."

"And you want me to protect the navy's image?"

"Of course. Certainly." He folded his hands and leaned forward. "This just turned out to be a huge mistake, as Ms. Beltower said."

"I said 'bogus,' Jules—no *mistake* about it."

Neal stood. "Captain Watembach, I'm sure you'll understand if I decline your invitation to pimp for the navy. I have a decision to make, though, that you should know about. Angela Vance expressed an interest in writing another book, nonfiction this time, about this case. She may need some inside help, you know, a technical adviser. Make sure she gets all the details right."

Neal headed for the door, followed by Lethajoy and Yvonne. "Good-bye, Captain," he said pleasantly as he drew the door open.

THE RAIN CONTINUED TO POUR as they left the legal center building, walking across the parking lot as quickly as Neal's injuries would allow.

"You're not getting within a hundred miles of that bitch Angela." Yvonne's tone clearly expressed her resolve.

Neal stopped and took her hand, giving it a kiss. "Sweetheart," he said, a grin spreading across his face, "I only said that for the captain's benefit. Let *him* sweat for a while." He gathered Yvonne to him, tipped his billed cap back and kissed her mouth.

Lethajoy watched from a few steps away. Neal reached out for her hand and drew her close to his side, enclosing both women. "How can I thank you enough, Lethajoy? And not just for winning the case—I mean for everything."

"First, you could let me get out of this rain," answered Lethajoy Beltower, Esq.